Inspiring Stories for Curious

Kids

Journeys Through Science

Sam Carter

© **Copyright 2024 - All rights reserved.**

ISBN: 978-969-53-9222-5

The content contained within this book may not be reproduced, duplicated, or transmitted without direct written permission from the author or the publisher.

Under no circumstances will any blame or legal responsibility be held against the publisher or author for any damages, reparation, or monetary loss due to the information contained within this book, either directly or indirectly.

Legal Notice:

This book is copyright-protected. It is only for personal use. You cannot amend, distribute, sell, use, quote, or paraphrase any part of the content within this book without the consent of the author or publisher.

Disclaimer Notice:

Please note the information contained within this document is for educational and entertainment purposes only. All effort has been executed to present accurate, up-to-date, reliable, and complete information. No warranties of any kind are declared or implied. Readers acknowledge that the author is not engaging in the rendering of legal, financial, medical, or professional advice. The content within this book has been derived from various sources. Please consult a licensed professional before attempting any techniques outlined in this book.

By reading this document, the reader agrees that under no circumstances is the author responsible for any losses, direct or indirect, that are incurred as a result of the use of the information contained within this document, including, but not limited to, errors, omissions, or inaccuracies

Your free bonus

As an additional BONUS for your purchase, I'd like to give you a gift:

BONUS: access to the Curious Young Readers YouTube Channel

When you buy this book, you also get access to the Curious Young Readers YouTube Channel.

This Channel can only be accessed after registering through the link below.

Get this bonus gift now:

https://curiousyoungreaders.com/bonus

Alternatively, scan the QR code below:

If you have any issues, disable your browser's adblocker for this page.

If that doesn't work, you can email me at sam@curiousyoungreaders.com

Contents

Introduction 7

Chapter One: The Universe and Beyond 10

    Story 1: The Comet Chasers 11

    Story 2: Voyaging to Mars 19

    Experiment 1: Exploring Comets 26

    Experiment 2: Solar System Exploration 29

Chapter Two: The Wonders of Our Planet 34

    Story 1: The Deepest Dive 36

    Story 2: The Dance of the Northern Lights 42

    Story 3: The Symphony of the Forest 48

    Experiment 1: Northern Lights Exploration 56

    Experiment 2: Ocean Exploration 59

Chapter Three: The Miracle of Life 63

    Story 1: The Butterfly's Secret 64

    Story 2: The Hidden World of Microbes 69

    Story 3: The Language of Whales 73

Experiment: The Transformation of a Butterfly 78

Experiment 2: Exploring the Microscopic World 81

Chapter Four: The Inventors and Their Inventions 86

Story 1: The Girl Who Played with Water..............................87

Story 2: The Code Breakers 92

Story 3: The Light of Edison...98

Experiment 1: The Journey of Invention 102

Experiment 2: 106

Chapter Five: The Power of Energy............................ 111

Story 1: The Sun's Gift 113

Story 2: The Wind that Powers the Future...........................121

Story 3: The Quest for Fusion...127

Experiment 1: Exploring Solar Energy 135

Experiment 2: Wind Energy..139

Chapter Six: Sports and Science 143

Story 1: The Science Behind the Perfect Swing 144

Story 2: Swimming With Science 152

Story 3: The Race Against Time...158

Experiment 1: 161

Conclusion 165

Bonus Experiments 168

Bonus Experiment 1: Balloon Rocket Science 168

Bonus Experiment 2: Homemade Lava Lamp 171

Bonus Experiment 3: Static Electricity Butterfly 173

Bonus Experiment 4: Invisible Ink 176

Bonus Experiment 5: Build a Simple Compass 178

Bonus Experiment 6: Rainbow in a Glass 180

Bonus Experiment 7: Salt Crystal Garden 183

Bonus Experiment 8: Soap-Powered Boat 185

Bonus Experiment 9: Bouncy Egg Experiment 187

Bonus Experiment 10: Oobleck (Non-Newtonian Fluid) 190

Bonus Experiment 11: Tornado in a Bottle 192

Bonus Experiment 12: Magnetic Slime 194

Bonus Experiment 13: Walking Water 196

Bonus Experiment 14: Grow Your Own Geode 199

Bonus Experiment 15: Egg Drop Challenge 201

Introduction

Are you ready to embark on an incredible journey through the wonders of science? Buckle up because we're about to blast off into a world filled with fascinating discoveries, mind-boggling experiments, and jaw-dropping facts that will leave you in awe!

In this book, you will discover a treasure trove of awe-inspiring stories about the universe, our magnificent planet Earth, the incredible web of life, and the crazy inventions that shape our world. But first, let me tell you why science is the coolest subject you'll ever learn!

Imagine this: You wake up one morning, stretch your arms, and peek out the window. What do you see? Maybe it's a bright blue sky with fluffy clouds drifting lazily by. Or perhaps it's a rainy day, and the pitter-patter of raindrops against the windowpane wakes you up.

Have you ever wondered why the sky is blue or how rainbows magically appear after a storm? Well, that's where science swoops in to save the day!

Science is like a superpower that helps us unlock the mysteries of the world around us. It is the key to endless possibilities and fuels our thirst for knowledge. Whether you're fascinated by the twinkling stars in the night sky, the bustling life in a drop of pond water, or the mind-boggling gadgets that make our lives easier, science has something for everyone.

But here's the best part: Science is more than memorizing facts and figures from dusty textbooks. It's about asking questions, observing, and diving headfirst into the unknown. It's about curiosity, creativity, and the thrill of discovery. So, if you've ever wondered why the sky is the limit or what makes the world go round (spoiler alert: it's not just gravity!), then you, my friend, are already a scientist in the making!

Now, let's talk about what you'll uncover in this book. Get ready to blast off into outer space and explore the far reaches of the universe, from glittering galaxies to mysterious black holes. Strap on your hiking boots as we trek through lush rainforests, scale towering mountains, and dive into the ocean's depths to uncover Earth's hidden gems. Prepare to marvel at the miracle of life as we journey from microscopic cells to towering trees, from busy bees to majestic whales.

We'll also meet the brilliant minds behind history's greatest inventions, from the humble wheel to the mind-boggling marvels of modern technology. So, whether you're dreaming of becoming an astronaut, a marine biologist, or the next Thomas Edison, something in these pages will fuel your passion for discovery.

So what are you waiting for? Turn the page, and the adventure begins! Who knows what wonders await us in the next chapter? There's only one way to find out. See you on the other side.

Chapter One: The Universe and Beyond

Get ready for a fantastic journey that goes beyond the limits of Earth! Have the stars ever mesmerized you and made you wonder about the secrets beyond our world? As we prepare to leave on a trip that will take us through the endlessness of space, where the impossible becomes possible and the unimaginable lies around every corner.

Imagine a playground where galaxies spin, stars shine, and planets twirl as they dance in space. This is not an ordinary place; it's one where reality isn't clear-cut, and the universe's wonders beg us to discover their secrets.

But hold on tight because we're not just here to take in the amazing show. No, we're getting ready for an exciting trip into the unknown, equipped with explorer gear and driven by joy and curiosity.

As we buckle up, we're about to embark on an exciting trip through the universe. We will unravel the mysteries of black holes, travel through the vast universe, and discover what faraway galaxies are hiding. The journey of learning and wonder never ends and starts right now.

Set our sights on the stars and let our thoughts run wild. We have already started our journey to discover the secrets of the universe, and we're about to dive right into the amazing things that await us in the vastness of space.

Are you all set? Let's enter a world where anything is possible!

Story 1: The Comet Chasers

A group of young explorers known as "The Comet Chasers" lived in a quaint town nestled amidst rolling hills. Guided by the passionate Dr. Ava, these aspiring scientists embarked on a mission to unravel the mysteries of the universe. With boundless curiosity and a thirst for knowledge, Dr. Ava and her team explored the enigmatic realm of space.

One starry night, as the town lay shrouded in the gentle embrace of darkness, Dr. Ava summoned her eager companions—Leo, the ingenious engineer; Maya, the intrepid pilot; and a cohort of aspiring astronomers—for an extraordinary journey. Their mission? To embark on a voyage into the cosmic unknown and study comets, those celestial wanderers that traverse the vastness of space.

As their spacecraft ascended into the boundless cosmos, Dr. Ava directed their gaze to the window, her voice filled with awe. "Behold, my friends," she exclaimed, "the universe's wonders laid bare before us. Each light twinkling represents a star, similar to our sun but within its cosmic realm. And that ethereal band stretching across the sky? It is the Milky Way, our celestial home, a tapestry of billions of stars and countless wonders."

Leo and Maya were captivated by the spectacle unfolding before them and marveled at the vastness of the cosmos. "It's like stepping into a realm of infinite possibilities," Leo mused, his voice tinged with wonder. "But how do we begin to unravel its secrets?"

With a knowing smile, Dr. Ava began unraveling the mysteries of the universe for her eager disciples. "Let us first ponder the nature of comets," she proposed, gesturing to a distant streak of light. Comets, my dear friends, are celestial nomads composed of ice, dust, and rocky debris. Originating from the icy depths of the outer solar system, they embark on cosmic journeys that bring them into the inner reaches, where they encounter the warming embrace of the sun."

Eager to delve deeper, the team leaned in as Dr. Ava continued her exposition. "As a comet draws near to the sun, the heat causes its icy core to sublime, releasing a mesmerizing array of gases and dust into space. This cosmic spectacle forms the characteristic tails that adorn comets, rendering them visible to observers on Earth and revealing insights into their composition and behavior."

Comets have fascinated humanity for centuries with their long, glowing tails and mysterious origins. These celestial travelers, often called "dirty snowballs" or "cosmic snowflakes," originate from the distant reaches of the solar system in a region known as the Oort Cloud. This vast reservoir of icy bodies lies beyond Neptune's orbit, extending trillions of kilometers into space.

As comets travel around our solar system, they can get pulled and pushed by planets' gravity like a ball bouncing in a pinball machine. This can change their paths and make them go in different directions. Some short-period comets have orbits that take them relatively close to the Sun and Earth. Because of this, we see them more often in our night sky, like regular visitors. Other comets, called long-period comets, take much more extended trips, sometimes lasting thousands or even millions of years before they come back around.

Throughout history, people from all over the world have seen comets streaking across the sky. In ancient times, they thought comets were unique signs from the gods or warnings of significant events. Some believed they signaled the birth or death of kings, the start of wars or times of hunger, or even a message from the gods that something important would happen. But now, with all our excellent science tools, like telescopes and space probes, we know that comets are super exciting things to study. They're not scary omens but fascinating objects that can teach us much about space!

With modern astronomy, scientists have learned so much about comets. We've sent spacecraft to visit them up close and even land on their icy surfaces. By studying comets, we've discovered that they're made of ice, dust, and rocky bits—the building blocks of our solar system. And when comets get closer to the Sun, the heat makes the ice turn into gas, creating those beautiful tails we see from Earth.

So, instead of being scared of comets, we can be excited to learn about them! They're like messengers from the distant reaches of space, carrying secrets and stories that help us understand our fantastic universe.

As their spacecraft traversed the cosmic expanse, the team marveled at the myriad wonders of the universe. They observed distant nebulae, the stellar nurseries where stars are born amidst clouds of gas and dust. They beheld star clusters, glittering jewels adorning the celestial canvas. They pondered the enigmatic presence of black holes, cosmic entities with gravitational pulls so strong that no light could escape their grasp.

A wealth of wonders await discovery in the vast expanse of space, from distant galaxies to mysterious black holes. But among all these celestial marvels, one of the most fascinating is the humble comet. A passionate astronomer, Dr. Ava shared stories with her team about some of the most famous comets from history, captivating their imaginations with tales of cosmic journeys and celestial spectacles.

One such comet was the Great Comet of 1680, a breathtaking sight that adorned the night sky with its magnificent tail stretching across the heavens. Imagine the awe and wonder it must have inspired in people who witnessed its celestial dance!

Then there's Halley's Comet, an actual cosmic celebrity that visits Earth-like clockwork every 76 years. Astronomers have observed and recorded its appearances for thousands of years, making it a celestial timekeeper and a source of fascination for generations. And who could forget Comet Shoemaker-Levy 9? In 1994, it made headlines when it collided with Jupiter in a spectacular display of cosmic fireworks, providing scientists with invaluable insights into the dynamics of our solar system.

Mia's curiosity bubbled over as Dr. Ava and her team gazed into the vast space. "Dr. Ava," she began, "what makes comets so special? They look amazing, but are they just pretty lights?"

Dr. Ava turned to Mia with a warm smile, her eyes gleaming excitedly. "Oh, Mia, comets are much more than just pretty lights," she exclaimed. "They're like time capsules, carrying secrets from the distant past!"

"Really?" Mia's eyes widened with wonder.

"Yes, indeed," Dr. Ava nodded eagerly. Comets are made of ice, dust, and rocky debris, much like the ingredients that formed our solar system billions of years ago."

Mia's brow furrowed in confusion. "But how do comets help us learn about the past?"

"Ah, that's where it gets interesting," Dr. Ava chuckled. "You see, comets travel through space in elliptical orbits, and sometimes, they swing by Earth, allowing us to study them up close. By analyzing the composition of cometary material, scientists can uncover clues about the conditions and events that shaped our cosmic neighborhood billions of years ago."

Mia's eyes sparkled with excitement. "That's amazing! But what else can we learn from comets?"

Dr. Ava's smile widened. "Well, comets' trajectories also offer valuable insights into the early solar system dynamics. Their elliptical orbits and periodic returns provide evidence of gravitational interactions and planetary migrations that occurred billions of years ago. By studying comet paths, scientists can piece together the ancient history of our solar system and trace the evolution of its planetary bodies over time."

Mia nodded thoughtfully. "Comets are like cosmic time travelers, carrying stories and secrets from long ago."

"Exactly!" Dr. Ava exclaimed. "And through their study, we can better understand the processes that have shaped our cosmic neighborhood over billions of years."

Mia's mind buzzed with newfound knowledge. "Wow, I never knew comets were so important! Thanks, Dr. Ava!"

Dr. Ava beamed with pride. "You're welcome, Mia. Remember, the universe is full of wonders waiting to be discovered, and comets are just the beginning of our cosmic journey."

At last, their quest led them to their destination—a new comet hurtling through the void with graceful abandon. "There it is!"

Maya exclaimed; her voice filled with excitement. "Our celestial quarry awaits!"

With Leo at the controls, they guided their spacecraft toward the comet, eager to witness its splendor up close. As they drew near, they marveled at the comet's nucleus, a pristine core surrounded by a luminous halo of gas and dust.

"It's a sight to behold," Leo whispered, his eyes transfixed by the celestial spectacle. "To think that we are here, bearing witness to the wonders of the cosmos!"

Having achieved their mission, Dr. Ava and her team returned to Earth, their hearts brimming with wonder and fascination. Though their journey had ended, their thirst for knowledge remained unquenched. "The universe is an endless wellspring of marvels," Dr. Ava declared. "With each discovery, we inch closer to unlocking its boundless secrets."

Whether you dream of exploring distant galaxies or gazing upon the stars from your backyard, the universe beckons with its infinite wonders. So, let us embrace the spirit of curiosity, embark on our cosmic odyssey, and journey into the mysteries of space. For in the vast expanse of the cosmos, there are wonders beyond imagination waiting to be revealed.

Story 2: Voyaging to Mars

In the middle of our solar system, a planet has captured the imagination of scientists and dreamers alike. It's called Mars and sits just beside Earth, far from the Sun. Mars has always been a bit mysterious—it's often called the "Red Planet" because of its rusty color, but there's so much more to it than that. Scientists have been studying Mars for a long time, trying to uncover its secrets and understand what makes it tick. And with each discovery, Mars reveals itself to be a truly fascinating world, full of wonder and mystery.

Humans have gazed at the rusty red orb in the night sky for centuries, pondering its secrets and dreaming of exploration. In the wondrous age of space exploration, these dreams became a reality with the incredible Mars rover missions.

Our story begins on Earth, where a team of brilliant scientists and engineers embarked on a mission to explore Mars like never before. Their goal was to send robotic explorers, known as rovers, to roam the Martian surface, gathering data and unraveling the planet's mysteries.

The first of these incredible robots was named Sojourner, and boy, was it a little powerhouse! Built by NASA, the American space agency, Sojourner was part of the Pathfinder mission, which blasted into space in 1996. This mission was no small feat; it required years of planning, testing, and collaboration between scientists, engineers, and researchers worldwide.

Now, picture this: Sojourner was like a tiny superhero, packed with gadgets and gizmos, ready to tackle the mysteries of Mars head-on. Its mission? Study Mars's atmosphere, climate, and even its rocky terrain! But how did Sojourner survive and thrive in such a harsh and alien environment?

After a seven-month journey through space, Sojourner and its companion lander, Pathfinder, touched down on the Martian surface on July 4, 1997. The world held its breath as the first images from Mars were beamed back to Earth, revealing a rocky, alien landscape unlike anything seen before. The successful landing was a testament to the incredible engineering and precision required for interplanetary exploration.

With its six wheels and advanced instruments, Sojourner was ready to roll. It wasted no time getting to work, using its onboard cameras and sensors to navigate the challenging terrain. The team back on Earth eagerly awaited each transmission, eager to learn more about Mars and its secrets.

One of Sojourner's primary tasks was to analyze the composition of rocks and soil on Mars. Using its Alpha Proton X-ray Spectrometer (APXS), Sojourner could determine the elements in these samples, providing valuable insights into the planet's geological history and potential for past or present life.

But Sojourner wasn't just a rock collector; it was also a weather reporter! Equipped with a meteorological station, Sojourner monitored Mars's temperature, wind speed, and atmospheric pressure. This data helped scientists better understand Mars's climate and how it differed from Earth's.

As Sojourner ventured across the Martian surface, it encountered challenges and surprises. From navigating rocky terrain to enduring dust storms, Sojourner demonstrated resilience and adaptability in a harsh and unforgiving environment.

For 83 days, Sojourner roamed the Martian surface, paving the way for future exploration and igniting humanity's fascination with the red planet. The world celebrated its discoveries and achievements, showcasing the incredible capabilities of robotic exploration and inspiring a new generation of scientists and space enthusiasts.

The legacy of Sojourner lives on, with its successors like Spirit, Opportunity, Curiosity, and Perseverance continuing the tradition of Martian exploration. Each new mission builds upon the knowledge and experiences gained from Sojourner, shaping our understanding of Mars and our place in the universe.

In the grand narrative of Mars exploration, the story continued after Sojourner. In the following years, NASA launched a series of increasingly advanced rovers, each pushing the boundaries of scientific discovery and human ingenuity.

In 2004, NASA embarked on an extraordinary mission by sending two rovers, Spirit and Opportunity, to explore opposite sides of the Martian landscape. Engineers built these intrepid robots with durability in mind, designing them to withstand the harsh Martian environment and operate effectively for 90 days. Yet, much to the astonishment of scientists and enthusiasts worldwide, Spirit and Opportunity surpassed their expected lifespans by far, with Opportunity setting an unprecedented record for the longest distance traveled by any rover on another celestial body.

Spirit and Opportunity made many groundbreaking discoveries throughout their extended missions. They stumbled upon compelling evidence of ancient water on Mars, a crucial finding suggesting that the planet once harbored a warmer and wetter climate conducive to sustaining life. The rovers tirelessly explored vast plains, scaled towering mountains, and delved into deep craters, unearthing valuable clues about Mars' geological history and environmental conditions, both past and present.

However, the Mars exploration saga continued to evolve with the launch of NASA's most ambitious rover—Curiosity. This rover, comparable in size to a small car, was equipped with an array of state-of-the-art instruments, including high-resolution cameras, spectrometers for chemical analysis, and even a drill capable of collecting rock samples from the Martian surface.

Curiosity's primary mission was nothing short of extraordinary: to search for tangible signs of past microbial life on Mars and to assess the planet's overall habitability for potential human exploration in the future. Over the years, Curiosity has lived up to its mission and then some. It has unearthed compelling evidence of ancient lakes, rivers, and deltas, providing tantalizing insights into Mars' geological past and environmental evolution. These discoveries have been pivotal in shaping our understanding of the red planet and its potential for supporting life, past or present.

Yet, the most captivating chapters of Curiosity's mission are to unfold. Looking ahead to the future of Mars exploration, NASA has planned even more ambitious missions, including the groundbreaking Perseverance rover launched in 2020. Equipped with an arsenal of cutting-edge scientific tools and instruments, Perseverance includes a groundbreaking sample collection system to gather and store Martian rock samples for future analysis. This rover's mission centers on meticulously examining the Martian surface in search of concrete evidence of ancient life, marking a significant leap forward in our quest to unravel the mysteries of Mars.

As we gaze toward the horizon of Mars exploration, one thing remains abundantly clear—the red planet holds boundless possibilities for discovery and adventure. With each new mission and technological advancement, we edge closer to unlocking the long-held secrets of this captivating world. And ultimately, as we peer deeper into the cosmos, we inch ever closer to answering one of humanity's most profound questions: Are we truly alone in the universe?

One of the most significant findings came from Opportunity's exploration of Meridiani Planum. Here, the rover discovered rocks containing hematite, a mineral that forms in water. This discovery provided compelling evidence that liquid water once flowed on the surface of Mars, suggesting that the planet may have once been habitable.

However, the most groundbreaking discovery came from Curiosity's exploration of Gale Crater, a massive impact basin that scientists believe was once filled with water. In 2013, Curiosity drilled into the Martian soil and found evidence of ancient organic molecules—the building blocks of life as we know it. While these molecules do not prove the existence of life on Mars, they provide tantalizing clues that the planet may have once harbored microbial life.

In addition to studying the Martian surface, Curiosity has also been monitoring the planet's atmosphere, searching for gases that could indicate the presence of life. In 2014, the rover detected a seasonal variation in methane levels, suggesting that the gas may be produced by biological processes deep beneath the Martian surface.

The most exciting part of Curiosity's mission is yet to come. In 2021, NASA's Perseverance rover touched down in Jezero Crater, an ancient lakebed that scientists believe may have once been home to microbial life. Equipped with state-of-the-art instruments, including a drill capable of collecting rock samples, Perseverance is on a mission to search for signs of ancient life and pave the way for future human exploration of Mars.

As we look to the future of Mars exploration, one thing is clear—the red planet holds endless possibilities for discovery and adventure. With each new mission, we come one step closer to unlocking the secrets of this fascinating world and answering the age-old question: Are we alone in the universe?

Experiment 1: Exploring Comets

Comets are fascinating celestial objects that have captured people's imaginations for centuries. They are made up of ice, dust, and rocky particles and travel through space, leaving behind a beautiful trail of gas and dust. In this experiment, we will recreate a comet's appearance and learn about its composition and behavior.

Be sure to ask a parent or guardian to join you and help you with this experiment. Safety first!

Materials Needed:

- Dry ice (available at some grocery stores or ice suppliers)
- Water
- Dirt or gravel

- A small bowl or container

- Protective gloves and goggles (to handle dry ice safely)

- A well-ventilated area (outdoors or in a spacious room)

Experiment Steps:

Step 1: Safety First

Before starting the experiment, put on your protective gloves and goggles. Dry ice is extremely cold and can cause frostbite if it comes into contact with bare skin. Always handle dry ice carefully and in a well-ventilated area to avoid inhaling too much carbon dioxide gas.

Step 2: Prepare the Comet Core

Fill a small bowl or container with water. This will represent the core of our comet. Place the container on a stable surface where it won't be disturbed.

Step 3: Add the "Dust" and "Rocky Particles"

Sprinkle dirt or gravel over the water's surface in the container. These particles represent the dust and rocky material in a comet's nucleus.

Step 4: Create the Comet Tail

Carefully place a piece of dry ice into the container with the water and dirt. Dry ice is frozen carbon dioxide, and when it comes into contact with warmer water, it will start to sublimate (turn directly from a solid to a gas). As the dry ice sublimates, it will release carbon dioxide gas, creating a visible trail that resembles a comet's tail.

Step 5: Observe and Learn

Watch as the dry ice reacts with the water and releases gas. A cloud forms above the water's surface, representing the gas and dust that trail behind a comet as it travels through space. Note how the gas moves and the patterns it creates in the air.

Step 6: Experiment with Different Conditions

You can try experimenting with different amounts of dry ice, water temperatures, and types of "dust" (e.g., sand and cocoa powder) to see how they affect the appearance of the comet's tail.

You can also try shining a flashlight on the comet to simulate the effect of sunlight on a real comet.

Step 7: Discuss and Reflect

After completing the experiment, take some time to discuss what you observed and learned. Talk about comets' composition, how they move through space, and why they develop a tail when approaching the sun. Encourage questions and curiosity, and explore additional resources to deepen your understanding of comets and other celestial objects.

You've successfully experimented to explore the fascinating world of comets. By recreating a comet's appearance and observing its behavior, you've gained valuable insights into the composition and behavior of these mysterious objects in space. Keep exploring and learning about the wonders of the universe!

Experiment 2: Solar System Exploration

Welcome, young astronomers, to an exciting journey through our solar system! In this experiment, we will explore the wonders of space and learn more about the planets, moons, and other celestial bodies that make up our cosmic neighborhood. Get ready to blast off into the unknown and discover the mysteries of the universe!

Materials Needed:

- Styrofoam balls (different sizes)
- Paints (various colors)
- Paintbrushes
- Wooden skewers
- Cardboard or foam board
- Scissors
- Tape
- Glue
- Marker pens
- Printed images or diagrams of the solar system (optional)

Experiment Steps:

Step 1: Prepare Your Materials

Gather all the materials above and set up a clean, well-lit workspace. Lay out the styrofoam balls, paints, paintbrushes, and wooden skewers for easy access.

Step 2: Research the Solar System

Before diving into the experiment, take some time to learn about the solar system. Read books or articles, watch educational videos, or explore online resources to familiarize yourself with the planets, their characteristics, and their positions in the solar system.

Step 3: Create the Sun

Start by painting one of the largest styrofoam balls yellow to represent the Sun. Use orange or red paint to add sunspots and other details to mimic the Sun's surface.

Step 4: Design the Planets

Next, choose different-sized Styrofoam balls to represent the solar system's planets. Use images or diagrams as references to paint each planet according to its unique features and colors:

- **Mercury**: A small grayish ball with craters and rocky terrain.
- **Venus**: A yellowish ball with swirling clouds and a rocky surface.
- **Earth**: A blue and green ball with oceans, continents, and white clouds.

- **Mars**: A reddish-orange ball with dusty terrain and polar ice caps.

- **Jupiter**: A large gas giant with bands of orange, brown, and white.

- **Saturn**: A gas giant with yellowish rings made from paper or foam.

- **Uranus**: A blue-green ball tilted on its side with faint rings.

- **Neptune**: A blue ball with dark blue spots and wispy clouds.

Feel free to get creative and add details such as mountains, valleys, or storms to make your planets more realistic.

Step 5: Assemble the Solar System

Once you have painted all the planets, use wooden skewers to attach them to a cardboard or foam board in the correct order from the Sun:

Mercury, Venus, Earth, Mars, Jupiter, Saturn, Uranus, Neptune.

Position each planet at varying distances from the Sun to represent its orbits around it. Use markers to label each planet and provide additional information about it.

Step 6: Explore and Learn

Now that your solar system model is complete, take some time to observe and study it. Move around the model to get a sense of the scale and relative sizes of the planets. Discuss their unique features, such as atmospheres, moons, and surface conditions.

Step 7: Reflect and Share

Reflect on what you have learned. After exploring the solar system model, reflect on what you have learned. Discuss any questions you have or interesting facts you discovered during the experiment. Consider sharing your model with friends or family and explaining what you have learned about the solar system.

Congratulations, young astronomers, on completing your journey through the solar system! By creating your model and exploring its features, you have gained valuable insights into the wonders of space and the celestial bodies that inhabit it. Keep exploring, asking questions, and seeking answers as you continue your scientific adventures. The universe is waiting to be discovered!

The mysteries of the universe are amazing, but there is still so much to explore on Earth. In the next chapter, you will explore our planet's wondrous events and mysteries.

Chapter Two: The Wonders of Our Planet

In a world filled with magic and mystery, a place of boundless beauty and wonder exists—a place we call home. Welcome, young adventurers, to a chapter dedicated to the awe-inspiring marvels of our planet Earth. From towering mountains to vast oceans, from lush rainforests to barren deserts, our planet is a treasure trove of diversity and enchantment waiting to be discovered.

Close your eyes for a moment and imagine standing atop a snow-capped peak, the crisp mountain air filling your lungs as you gaze at a panorama of breathtaking vistas. Or picture yourself diving into the ocean's depths, surrounded by vibrant coral reefs teeming with life in every hue imaginable. This, dear readers, is just a glimpse of the wonders that await us as we embark on our journey into the heart of our planet.

But why should we explore Earth's wonders? The answer lies in our planet's endless opportunities for learning and discovery. From understanding the delicate balance of ecosystems to marveling at the forces that shape our landscapes, every step we take on this journey brings us closer to unlocking our world's secrets.

So, fasten your seatbelts and prepare for an adventure unlike any other. In the following chapters, we will embark on a voyage of exploration, delving deep into our planet's wonders and uncovering the mysteries beneath its surface. From the smallest microorganisms to the grandest geological formations, we will learn about the intricate web of life that sustains us and the remarkable processes that have shaped our planet over millions of years.

But our journey will not be just about learning facts and figures. Along the way, we will discover the importance of conservation and stewardship as we strive to protect and preserve the precious ecosystems that make our planet unique. Through our exploration, we will understand the interconnectedness of all living things and the vital role that each of us plays in ensuring the health and vitality of our planet for generations to come.

So, young adventurers, are you ready to embark on this journey with me? Together, let us explore our planet's wonders, marvel at its beauty, and celebrate the incredible diversity of life that calls Earth home. For in the vast tapestry of the cosmos, there is no place quite like our own blue-green planet—a place of wonder, discovery, and endless possibility.

Story 1: The Deepest Dive

In the vast expanse of the Pacific Ocean, there lay a hidden world of wonder and mystery—the Mariana Trench. This deep, dark abyss, shrouded in secrecy, beckoned to explorers and scientists, daring them to uncover its secrets. And so, the adventure of "The Deepest Dive" began.

Our story begins with a team of intrepid explorers led by the fearless Dr. Emily, a marine biologist with a passion for uncovering the mysteries of the deep sea. Alongside her were her trusty companions—Jake, the adventurous diver; Maya, the brilliant engineer; and Max, the curious oceanographer. Together, they set out on a daring expedition to explore the depths of the Mariana Trench, armed with cutting-edge technology and boundless curiosity.

As their submarine descended into the inky depths, the team marveled at the eerie beauty of the ocean floor. Strange and otherworldly creatures drifted past their viewport, their bioluminescent glow illuminating the darkness. Dr. Emily explained to her companions that these creatures had adapted to survive in the extreme conditions of the deep sea, where sunlight could not penetrate, and pressure was crushing.

"Did you know," Dr. Emily's voice resonated through the submarine's cabin, "that we've only explored a tiny fraction of the ocean floor? There are vast swathes of uncharted territory down here, teeming with life and waiting to be discovered."

Jake's eyes widened with wonder as he leaned closer to the viewport, trying to peer into the darkness surrounding them. The ocean's depths stretched endlessly, hiding untold mysteries beneath its surface. "What else could be hiding down here?" he wondered aloud, his voice filled with excitement and anticipation.

"We are not sure, which is so exciting! We get to explore and make discoveries right here on Earth."

As the team descended into the Mariana Trench, the deepest part of the ocean, they encountered many strange and wondrous sights at every turn. Towering underwater mountains, known as seamounts, rose majestically from the ocean floor, their peaks obscured by the murky depths. Dr. Emily's eyes sparkled with enthusiasm as she explained the remarkable geological processes that created the towering seamounts scattered across the ocean floor.

"Imagine, if you will," she began, gesturing animatedly to the submarine's viewport, "that beneath the ocean's surface lies a vast network of tectonic plates—gigantic puzzle pieces that fit together to form the Earth's crust. These plates are constantly in motion, albeit at an invisible pace. When two plates collide, one may be forced beneath the other in subduction. As the subducted plate descends into the Earth's mantle, it heats up and melts, forming magma. Under tremendous pressure, this magma rises towards the surface, eventually breaking through and forming volcanoes."

She paused momentarily, allowing her words to sink in before continuing.

"Now, imagine that instead of rising to the surface, the magma gets stuck beneath the crust, creating a bulge or swelling in the ocean floor. Over millions of years, as more magma accumulates and the bulge grows larger, it eventually breaches the surface, forming a volcanic island. However, as the volcanic activity subsides and the island erodes, a towering underwater mountain known as a seamount remains."

Jake's eyes widened with understanding as he absorbed Dr. Emily's explanation. "So, these seamounts are like hidden mountains beneath the waves!" he exclaimed, his excitement palpable.

"Exactly!" Dr. Emily replied with a smile. "And not only are these seamounts marvels of geological engineering, but they also serve as crucial habitats for various marine life. The nutrient-rich waters surrounding these underwater mountains provide a fertile environment for plankton and other small organisms, attracting larger predators such as fish, sharks, and whales. In this way, seamounts play a vital role in the health and biodiversity of the ocean ecosystem."

But it wasn't just the seamounts that captured their attention. They also witnessed fields of hydrothermal vents, where hot, mineral-rich water spewed from the Earth's crust, creating oases of life in the otherwise barren depths. These hydrothermal vents, Dr. Emily explained, were like underwater geysers, formed by the heat of the Earth's mantle melting the surrounding rock and releasing trapped gases and minerals. Despite the extreme conditions, these hydrothermal vents were home to a thriving ecosystem of unique and bizarre creatures adapted to survive in the harsh environment.

However, they encounter a hidden cavern within the trench walls. Inside, they found a thriving ecosystem, unlike anything they had ever seen. Strange creatures adapted to survive in extreme darkness and pressure roamed the cavern floor, and their alien forms were a testament to the resilience of life.

As they explored further, Maya, the engineer, pointed out the intricate networks of caves and tunnels that crisscrossed the cavern walls. "These caves could be home to even more undiscovered species," she said, her voice filled with excitement. "Who knows what secrets they may hold?"

Dr. Emily's eyes sparkled with excitement as she surveyed the scene before her. "This is just the beginning," she said, her voice filled with wonder. "Who knows what other secrets lie hidden within the ocean?"

As the team's submarine went deeper into the Mariana Trench, a place very few people have been to, they found many amazing things that helped them learn more about the ocean's secrets. With each discovery, their interest grew, pushing them to see more of the fantastic things hidden under the water.

One amazing thing they found was a type of bioluminescent jellyfish that no one had ever seen before. Its ethereal glow lit up the deep sea. These jellyfish swam smoothly through the water. The light that pulsed through their clear bodies looked like it came from another world. Dr. Emily was amazed by how beautiful these creatures were and said that their bioluminescence was probably a way for them to communicate or hide in the dark where sunlight couldn't reach.

As the team went deeper into the trench, they came across a huge field of deep-sea vents surrounded by a crazy community of strange living things. Dr. Emily said these vents were like oases underwater because they provided food and warmth for the animals. Giant tube worms with bodies over six feet long and strange shrimp without eyes that crawled across the ocean floor looking for food lived there.

They found a secret cave inside the trench walls, probably the most fantastic thing they found. What the team saw inside was amazing—an environment alive and well like nothing they had ever seen. Strange and otherworldly creatures roamed the tunnel floor. Their strange shapes showed how life can survive in the deep sea's harsh conditions.

There were ghostly white octopuses living in the tunnel. Their bodies were clear and blended in with the water around them. These elusive animals were great at hiding. They could change color and texture at the touch of a button to blend in with their surroundings. Maya, the engineer, was amazed at how well they were able to adapt to their surroundings. She pointed out that they had to be able to hide from enemies in order to stay alive.

As the team's submarine continued its descent into the depths of the Mariana Trench, Dr. Emily's explanation lingered in their minds, adding another layer of understanding to the wonders they encountered below. And as they gazed out into the vast expanse of the ocean floor, they couldn't help but marvel at the incredible forces of nature that shaped the world around them.

As their expedition drew to a close and the team returned to the surface, they couldn't help but feel a sense of awe and wonder at the world they had uncovered. The Mariana Trench, with its dark depths and mysterious inhabitants, the Mariana Trench had captured their imaginations and left them hungry for more.

Story 2: The Dance of the Northern Lights

In a quiet town nestled among snow-capped mountains and dense forests, excitement brewed in the crisp winter air. It was a special night when the heavens would come alive with a magical display known as the Northern Lights.

Mia, a curious twelve-year-old girl with bright eyes and a heart full of wonder, stood in the town square alongside her grandmother, Nana June. They joined the townsfolk, their faces upturned towards the night sky, eagerly awaiting the spectacle to unfold.

As the sun dipped below the horizon, painting the sky with hues of pink and orange, a collective gasp swept through the crowd. A faint, ethereal glow began to shimmer on the northern horizon, growing brighter and more vibrant by the second. Mia's heart fluttered with excitement as she watched, her eyes wide with wonder.

"Look, Mia," Nana June whispered, her voice filled with awe, "it's the Aurora Borealis—the Northern Lights."

Mia's gaze remained fixed on the dancing ribbons of light as they swirled and twirled across the sky. She had heard stories of the Northern Lights—how they painted the heavens with colors beyond imagination. Still, nothing could have prepared her for the breathtaking beauty unfolding before her eyes.

"Nana," Mia whispered, her voice barely above a hush, "what are the Northern Lights? How do they happen?"

Nana June smiled warmly, her eyes twinkling with knowledge passed down through generations. "Ah, Mia," she began, "the

Northern Lights are a magical phenomenon caused by interactions between the Earth's magnetic field and particles from the sun."

Mia's brow furrowed in confusion. "Particles from the sun? What do you mean, Nana?"

Nana June chuckled softly, delighted by Mia's curiosity. "Well, Mia, the sun is not just a source of light and warmth—it's also a giant ball of energy. Sometimes, it releases bursts of this energy into space, in a phenomenon known as solar flares."

Mia's eyes widened with fascination. "Solar flares? What happens to them?"

"When these solar flares reach Earth," Nana June continued, "they release charged particles—tiny bits of energy—that hurtle towards our planet at incredible speeds."

Mia nodded, beginning to grasp the concept. "And what happens when these particles reach Earth?"

Nana June smiled, her eyes sparkling with excitement. "That's where the magic begins, Mia. You see, Earth has its protective shield—a magnetic field—that surrounds our planet like an invisible forcefield. When these charged particles from the sun collide with the Earth's magnetic field, they are directed towards the poles—either the North Pole or the South Pole—where the magnetic field is strongest."

Mia's imagination soared as she pictured the charged particles racing toward the poles, painting the sky with colors unseen. "And what happens next, Nana?"

"As these charged particles travel towards the Earth's poles," Nana June explained, "they collide with gases in the atmosphere—mostly nitrogen and oxygen—causing them to light up in a dazzling display of colors. The result is the Northern Lights—a mesmerizing dance of light and color that illuminates the night sky."

Mia's heart swelled with wonder as she watched the Northern Lights perform their celestial ballet. She had never imagined something so magical could exist in the world, right here in her backyard.

"And how long do the Northern Lights last, Nana?" Mia asked, her voice filled with curiosity.

Nana June smiled, her eyes crinkling at the corners. "The duration of the Northern Lights can vary, Mia. Sometimes, they last for just a few minutes, while other times, they can dance across the sky for hours on end. It all depends on factors like the strength of the solar flares and the Earth's magnetic field."

Mia nodded, her mind buzzing with newfound knowledge. She had always loved science, but seeing the Northern Lights with her own eyes had ignited a passion within her—a desire to understand the mysteries of the universe and explore the wonders that lay beyond.

Mia felt awe and wonder as she gazed at the shimmering ribbons of light painting the night sky. She had learned so much from Nana June's explanation, but there was still much more to discover about the Northern Lights.

"Nana," Mia said, her voice filled with excitement, "do the Northern Lights happen only on Earth? Or do other planets also have their version of the Northern Lights?"

Nana June's eyes sparkled with pride at Mia's curiosity. "That's an excellent question, Mia," she replied. "While the Northern Lights, also known as the Aurora Borealis, occur primarily near the North Pole, there is a similar phenomenon near the South Pole called the Aurora Australis. And yes, other planets in our solar system, such as Jupiter and Saturn, also experience auroras, albeit with their unique characteristics."

Mia's mind whirled with possibilities as she imagined the beauty of auroras on distant planets. She couldn't wait to learn more about these celestial phenomena and the science behind them.

"Nana," Mia said, her voice filled with determination, "I want to learn everything there is to know about the Northern Lights and auroras. Will you help me?"

Nana June's heart swelled with pride at Mia's eagerness to learn. "Of course, my dear," she replied, affectionately squeezing Mia's hand. "Together, we'll explore the wonders of the universe and uncover the secrets of the Northern Lights. Who knows what adventures await us?"

As the night wore on, Mia and Nana June remained in the town square, watching in awe as the Northern Lights continued to dance overhead. As they finally made their way home, Mia couldn't help but feel grateful for the experience. This experience opened her eyes to the beauty of the natural world and sparked a lifelong curiosity for the wonders of the universe.

As the night wore on, Mia and Nana June remained in the town square, watching in awe as the Northern Lights continued to dance overhead. As they finally made their way home, Mia couldn't help but feel grateful for the experience. This experience opened her eyes to the beauty of the natural world and sparked a lifelong curiosity for the wonders of the universe.

Story 3: The Symphony of the Forest

A young biologist named Maya set out on a trip unlike any other. She went to the middle of the Amazon rainforest, where sunlight filters through the thick canopy and the air smells like earth and plants. Maya went deep into the environment with her trusty notebook and a sense of wonder in her heart. She was eager to learn its secrets and understand how the complex web of life that lived there worked.

As she went deeper into the forest, Maya was amazed by the rainbow of colors and sounds around her. Birds of every color flew through the trees, and their sweet songs could be heard through the sky. Butterflies flew on the wind, and the light reflecting off their tiny wings made them sparkle.

Maya pulled out her journal to log her findings.

Day 1:

Today was the start of my adventure into the Amazon rainforest, and it was truly awe-inspiring. The Amazon, known as the "lungs of the Earth," is the largest tropical rainforest globally and one of the most biodiverse ecosystems. Upon entering this vibrant setting,

I was welcomed by a chorus of sounds—a mix of birdsong, insects buzzing, and the soft rustling of leaves. The overwhelming environment showcased the diverse life thriving in the lush surroundings.

As I walked through the forest trail, the tall trees above me filled me with awe. These massive trees are crucial to the rainforest, offering vital resources like food, shelter, and habitat for numerous species. From the top layer of the rainforest, where the tallest trees grow, to the lower layer, where smaller plants and shrubs thrive in the sunlight filtering through the trees, every level is a whole of life, each contributing to the complex ecosystem.

As I explored the heart of the Amazon, I came across a wide variety of wildlife, each more captivating than the previous one. The canopy was alive with vibrant parrots and toucans, their colorful feathers against the lush green backdrop. Jaguars crept through the undergrowth, their golden coats blending in with the shadows. Above, sloths relaxed in the branches, moving slowly to reflect the leisurely rainforest life.

What stood out to me was how everything in the Amazon is connected. Every species, whether tiny insects or big predators, has a vital part in preserving the fragile harmony of the ecosystem. Every interaction within these ancient forests sustains a vibrant tapestry of life, from pollination to seed dispersal, predation to decomposition.

As I navigated the Amazon, I felt a strong need to document and research the amazing variety of life around me. I diligently documented my findings on the animals' behaviors and adaptations, and I am excited to enhance our knowledge of this exceptional ecosystem.

The Amazon rainforest is a hub of biodiversity and provides essential resources and ecosystem services. It is vital to maintaining life on Earth, supplying oxygen, regulating the climate, and supporting indigenous communities. Nevertheless, it is encountering significant challenges due to deforestation, climate change, and unsustainable land use practices.

As I explore the Amazon, I feel a solid duty to safeguard this incredible wilderness for future generations. By recording its marvels, we can motivate others to act and protect this unique ecosystem for future generations.

Day 2:

Today was another exciting day spent in the Amazon rainforest, and I couldn't help but be amazed by the vast variety of plant life around me. As I explored the forest, I stumbled upon a sunlit clearing with tall trees reaching up to the sky and vibrant colors all around. The variety of plant species was impressive, ranging from tall canopy trees to delicate ferns and colorful flowers, each contributing to the complex web of life that supports the rainforest ecosystem.

The tall trees in the canopy were impressive, standing over 100 feet high. These large trees play a crucial role in the rainforest ecosystem by offering shelter to various animals, absorbing carbon dioxide, and producing oxygen. Among the Amazon's most famous trees are the towering kapok tree, whose massive trunk reaches up to 10 feet in diameter, and the majestic Brazil nut tree, known for producing the largest seeds in the region.

Strolling through the forest trail, I was mesmerized by the dense undergrowth covering the ground. A thick layer of ferns, mosses, and other small plants blanketed the ground, forming a lush green landscape. These plants are essential for nutrient cycling and soil formation, supporting the diverse life in the rainforest.

One of the best parts of my day was discovering a chattering stream winding through the woods. The water was clear and sparkling in the sunlight, with colorful fish darting among the rocks below. These streams play a crucial role for numerous species in the rainforest, offering a vital supply of fresh water for various purposes. They are essential pathways for wildlife, enabling animals to move through the forest and reach multiple parts of their habitat.

Later that day, I had the opportunity to watch a group of monkeys gracefully swinging through the trees. These nimble animals are well-suited to the rainforest environment, thanks to their long limbs and tails help them move effortlessly through the thick canopy. I observed amazement as they searched for food, interacted with each other using various calls and gestures, and played with endless energy. This highlighted the vast array of life in the Amazon rainforest and the significance of safeguarding this delicate ecosystem for future generations.

Day 3:

Today, I had the extraordinary privilege of witnessing one of the most enchanting events in the Amazon rainforest—the blooming of the giant water lilies, also known as Victoria amazonica. These remarkable flowers, named after Queen Victoria of England, are renowned for their immense size and stunning beauty.

The Victoria amazonica blooms for just one night each year, making the moment all the more special. As the sun set and darkness descended upon the rainforest, I went to a serene pond where these magnificent lilies were known to reveal their splendor.

As I stood by the water's edge, anticipation coursed through me, knowing I was about to witness a spectacle of nature like no other. And then, as if on cue, the first delicate petals began to unfurl, their pristine white color illuminated by the soft glow of the moon above.

Each petal seemed to glow with an otherworldly radiance, casting shimmering reflections on the pond's mirror-like surface. The sheer size of the lilies was astounding, with leaves that spanned several feet in diameter, creating a mesmerizing display of natural grandeur.

But it wasn't just their size that left me in awe—it was also their intricate structure and remarkable adaptation to their environment. The giant water lilies have evolved to thrive in the Amazon rainforest's unique conditions, with leaves specially designed to support their weight and float effortlessly on the water's surface.

As I gazed upon the blooming lilies, I couldn't help but marvel at nature's ingenuity. These beautiful flowers serve as a source of wonder and inspiration and an integral part of the rainforest ecosystem. They provide shelter and food for various aquatic creatures, from tiny fish to frogs and insects, contributing to the rich biodiversity of the Amazon.

Witnessing the blooming of the giant water lilies was a moment I will never forget—a reminder of the beauty and resilience of the natural world and the importance of protecting it for generations to come.

Day 4:

Today, I had the incredible privilege of witnessing a phenomenon that few people ever see—a gathering of butterflies known as a "butterfly tornado." As I ventured deeper into the Amazon rainforest, I noticed a swirling mass of color ahead. As I drew closer, I realized it was a massive swarm of butterflies, fluttering and swirling in a mesmerizing dance.

The butterflies were a kaleidoscope of colors, with wings of every hue imaginable. Some were vibrant shades of red and orange, while others shimmered with iridescent blues and greens. It was a breathtaking sight, and its sheer beauty transfixed me.

But the butterfly tornado wasn't just a stunning spectacle—it was also a testament to the incredible biodiversity of the Amazon rainforest. The Amazon is home to an astonishing array of butterfly species, each uniquely adapted to its environment. From the smallest, most delicate butterflies to the largest and most majestic, the rainforest teems with life in all its forms.

As I watched the butterflies dance through the air, I couldn't help but marvel at the intricacy of nature's design. These delicate creatures play a crucial role in the ecosystem, pollinating flowers and plants and serving as a vital food source for other animals.

But their beauty belies the challenges they face in an ever-changing world. Deforestation, climate change, and habitat loss threaten the delicate balance of the Amazon rainforest, putting the future of its inhabitants—including the butterflies—at risk.

I reflect on my time in the Amazon, filled with wonder and gratitude for the incredible diversity of life that calls this place home. It's a reminder of the importance of preserving our natural world and protecting the delicate balance of ecosystems like the Amazon for future generations to enjoy.

Experiment 1: Northern Lights Exploration

Are you ready to embark on a thrilling journey to uncover the secrets of the Northern Lights? With this awesome experiment, you'll learn how these mesmerizing lights are formed in the sky. Don't forget to grab a parent or guardian to help you!

Materials Needed:

- Clear glass or plastic container (like a fish tank or large jar)
- Water
- Cooking oil
- Small flashlight or LED light
- Black paper or cardboard
- Tape
- Magnetic wand or magnet
- Optional: Food coloring (for extra fun!)

Experiment Steps:

Step 1: Set Up Your Exploration Zone

First things first, find a nice spot to conduct your experiment. Lay out all your materials on a clean, flat surface, and get ready to dive into the world of science!

Step 2: Create the Earth's Atmosphere

Fill your clear container with water, leaving a little space at the top. Now, carefully pour a thin layer of cooking oil onto the water's surface. This oil layer will be like Earth's atmosphere, so make sure it covers the water evenly.

Step 3: Design Your Miniature Landscape

Let's get creative! Cut out some cool shapes from the black paper or cardboard—think trees, mountains, or anything else you like. Stick these shapes to the sides of your container using tape. This will create a silhouette against the background.

Step 4: Let the Solar Wind Blow

Time to simulate the solar wind—the stream of charged particles from the sun that causes the Northern Lights. Turn off the lights in the room and shine your flashlight or LED light into the container from one side. Move the light around to mimic the movement of the solar wind through space.

Step 5: Observe the Oil Patterns

Watch closely as the light shines into the container. See how the oil on the water's surface reacts to the light. You might notice some astonishing patterns forming—these represent the interaction between the solar wind and Earth's magnetic field!

Step 6: Add Some Magnetic Magic

Now, let's introduce Earth's magnetic field. Use your magnetic wand or magnet to create a magnetic field within the container. Move the magnet around the outside of the container to simulate Earth's magnetic field. Notice how the oil reacts to the magnetic field—it's like magic!

Step 7: Optional: Splash of Color

Add a few drops of food coloring to the water for an extra fun touch before adding the oil.

Different colors can represent different gases in Earth's atmosphere and make your experiment even more colorful and exciting!

Step 8: Reflect and Learn Together

Once you've finished the experiment, chat with your parent or guardian about what you observed and learned. Ask questions, share your thoughts, and explore more about the fantastic Northern Lights together. Who knows what other mysteries of the universe you'll uncover next?

You've just completed an incredible experiment exploring the science behind the Northern Lights. Keep up the curiosity and continue exploring the wonders of our world. Who knows? Maybe one day, you'll be the one making groundbreaking discoveries about our world and beyond!

Experiment 2: Ocean Exploration

In this experiment, we will dive deep into the ocean's mysteries to explore its fascinating inhabitants and learn more about its diverse ecosystems. Get ready to discover the wonders of marine life and unlock the secrets of the deep sea!

Materials Needed:
- Large clear plastic container or fish tank

- Water (preferably filtered or distilled)
- Ocean-themed toys or figurines (e.g., plastic sea creatures)
- Sand or gravel
- Rocks or seashells
- Magnifying glass
- Thermometer
- pH test strips
- Oceanography books or educational resources (optional)

Experiment Steps:

Step 1: Set Up Your Ocean Habitat

Begin by filling the large clear plastic container or fish tank with water. Make sure the container is clean and free from any contaminants. Add sand or gravel to the bottom of the container to create a natural substrate for your ocean habitat. Arrange rocks or seashells to mimic underwater features such as reefs or caves.

Step 2: Add Ocean Creatures

After setting up your habitat, populate it with ocean-themed toys or figurines representing various marine creatures. Choose diverse animals, including fish, sharks, whales, dolphins, turtles, and invertebrates like jellyfish and octopuses. Arrange the creatures in different areas of the habitat to simulate their natural habitats and interactions.

Step 3: Observe and Explore

Using a magnifying glass, carefully observe the creatures in your ocean habitat. Note their colors, shapes, sizes, and behaviors. Use reference materials or books to identify species and learn more about their characteristics and habitats. Pay attention to how they move, eat, and interact with one another.

Step 4: Measure Water Parameters

To understand the conditions of your ocean habitat, use a thermometer to measure the water temperature. Record the temperature in degrees Celsius or Fahrenheit. Next, use pH test strips to measure the water's acidity or alkalinity. Dip the test strip into the water and compare the color change to the pH scale provided with the test strips.

Step 5: Learn About Ocean Ecosystems

Take some time to read books or educational resources about oceanography and marine biology. Learn about ocean ecosystems, including coral reefs, kelp forests, open ocean, and deep sea.

Discover the unique plants and animals that inhabit each ecosystem and their critical roles in maintaining the ocean's health.

Step 6: Create a Marine Food Web

Using your knowledge of ocean ecosystems, create a marine food web to illustrate the relationships between different organisms. Identify producers (e.g., phytoplankton), consumers (e.g., fish, sharks), and decomposers (e.g., bacteria). Draw or label a diagram showing how energy flows through the food web, starting with sunlight as the primary energy source.

Step 7: Reflect and Share

After exploring your ocean habitat and learning about marine life, take some time to reflect on your experience. Discuss any interesting discoveries you made or questions you have about the ocean. Consider sharing your findings with friends or family and encouraging them to join the exploration.

By diving into the ocean's depths and observing its inhabitants, you have gained valuable insights into the wonders of marine life and the importance of ocean conservation. Keep exploring, learning, and protecting our oceans for future generations to enjoy!

Chapter Three: The Miracle of Life

You are about to embark on an exciting journey through life's wonders. Have you ever considered how many different kinds of life live on Earth? What do these tiny creatures do to keep the planet's delicate balance? Take off on the wings of a butterfly. What secrets hide in its elegant flap? What can we learn from the strange language whales use to find their way across the oceans?

In this exciting chapter, we set sail on a thrilling journey to find the answers to these and other exciting questions. Get ready to explore the fantastic range of life on Earth, from the minuscule world of bacteria to the grand worlds of birds in the sky and whales that live in the ocean. We'll learn about the interesting stories of survival, change, and connection that hold life together.

Come with us as we try to unravel nature's secrets and discover the amazing things happening around us daily. Are you ready to become an adventurous explorer and experience the amazing things in life for yourself? The trip is coming up, and it will be nothing short of amazing!

Story 1: The Butterfly's Secret

In a bustling garden teeming with life, a group of curious kids embarked on a wondrous journey into the magical world of butterflies. It all began with a small egg delicately laid by a female butterfly on the underside of a leaf. Little did they know that within this tiny egg lay the beginnings of a remarkable transformation that would take this tiny creature on a journey of growth and change.

Day 1:

The children were captivated by the egg's beauty as they examined it closely. The fragile shell was decorated with detailed patterns, resembling a small work of art created by nature. Every twist and turn glistened in the sunlight, creating captivating shadows on the leaf below.

They were amazed by the fragile structure of the egg and how such a tiny thing could contain the potential for new life. The egg seemed like a small treasure chest, ready to be opened to unveil its valuable contents. Unbeknownst to them, inside this seemingly regular egg was the potential for something remarkable—a change that would capture their hearts and spark their imaginations.

Day 3:

After careful observation, the egg began to hatch after a few days, revealing a tiny caterpillar nestled inside. At first glance, the caterpillar appeared small and unassuming, but the kids knew that within its humble exterior lay the potential for something truly extraordinary.

The caterpillar wasted no time exploring its surroundings, eagerly devouring the leaves of the plant on which it was born. It grew larger and stronger with each bite, shedding its skin several times as it outgrew its old body. This rapid growth and change was a testament to these remarkable creatures' incredible resilience and adaptability.

Day 7:

As time passed, the children were amazed by the caterpillar's incredible transformation, which showcased the beauty of nature unfolding before their eyes. They watched as the caterpillar stopped eating and wrapped itself in silken thread to create a protective chrysalis shell. They discovered that the chrysalis provided a secure place for the caterpillar to transform remarkably.

Out of sight, the caterpillar began a transformative journey within the chrysalis. They found that the caterpillar's body turned into a soupy substance through liquefaction, breaking its tissues into individual cells. The kids were captivated by the discovery that specialized cells known as imaginal discs, dormant since the caterpillar's embryonic stage, started to awaken and multiply within the liquid mass.

Imaginal discs are like magic blueprints hidden within a caterpillar's body, waiting for the right moment to burst into action. When the caterpillar forms a chrysalis, these discs work, building the intricate body parts of a beautiful butterfly.

Gradually, these cells guided the development of the butterfly's body, such as its wings, legs, antennae, and other detailed characteristics. The caterpillar transformed into a beautiful butterfly during this cellular differentiation and growth.

Day 14:

After two weeks of patient waiting, the chrysalis began to wiggle and shake, signaling the butterfly's emergence. With bated breath, the kids watched the chrysalis split open, revealing a delicate butterfly unfolding its wings for the first time. It was a moment of pure magic as the butterfly stretched its wings, its vibrant colors catching the sunlight in a dazzling display.

As the butterfly took flight for the first time, the kids couldn't help but feel a sense of wonder and awe. It reminded them of the incredible beauty and complexity of the natural world, a world filled with marvels waiting to be discovered and explored.

Butterflies are truly remarkable creatures, unlike any other insects in the animal kingdom. One of the most fascinating aspects of butterflies is their wings. Did you know that butterfly wings are covered in tiny scales? These scales give butterflies vibrant colors and patterns, making each unique. Butterflies (and moths) are the only insects with scales covering their wings!

Butterflies also have an incredible sense of time and direction. They can track the sun's position and use it to navigate the world. This ability is crucial for their survival, allowing them to find food, mates, and suitable habitats.

And here's a fun fact: butterflies taste with their feet! When they land on a flower, they use their feet to taste the nectar to ensure it's sweet and delicious. It's like having a built-in taste tester wherever they go!

A group of butterflies is sometimes called a flutter, and it's easy to see why. Watching a group of butterflies flit and flutter through the air is a truly mesmerizing sight, a testament to the beauty and grace of these remarkable creatures.

Butterflies also have some of the most amazing eyes in the insect world. Their eyes are made up of thousands of tiny lenses, allowing them to see in almost every direction at once. This gives them a 360-degree view of their surroundings, helping them to spot predators and find food.

But perhaps most fascinating of all is the butterfly's diet. Unlike many other insects, butterflies enjoy an all-liquid diet. They sip nectar from flowers using their long, straw-like tongues called proboscis. But they don't just drink nectar—they also enjoy sipping on other liquids like tree sap and even mud puddles!

So, the next time you see a butterfly fluttering by, take a moment to appreciate the incredible journey it took to get there. From a tiny egg to a beautiful butterfly, each one is a marvel of nature's design, reminding us of the magic and wonder that surrounds us daily.

Story 2: The Hidden World of Microbes

Welcome to the mesmerizing world of microbes, where the tiniest creatures wield extraordinary power! Imagine creatures so minuscule they're invisible to the naked eye, yet they hold sway over the very fabric of life itself. These microbes exist all around us, inhabiting the air we breathe, the water we drink, the soil beneath our feet, and even inside our bodies!

Microbes are so tiny that they're impossible to see without a microscope. Despite their diminutive size, they are living organisms with immense significance. Among them are bacteria, viruses, fungi, and protozoa play a vital role in shaping our world. From breaking down organic matter in the soil to help us digest food in our stomachs, and microbes are the unsung heroes of our environment.

They may be tiny, but don't let their size fool you—microbes are mighty. They profoundly impact ecosystem health, our bodies' vitality, and even history's course. So, the next time you marvel at the wonders of the world around you, and remember to acknowledge the incredible influence of these unseen champions—the microbes!

Microbes come in all shapes and sizes, and each type has a special job. Bacteria are tiny single-celled creatures that can look like tiny balls, rods, or spirals under a microscope. Some bacteria are helpful and do things like help plants grow or help us digest our food. Others can make us sick if they get inside our bodies.

Viruses are tinier than bacteria and are not considered living things because they can't grow or reproduce independently. Instead, they must invade other living cells to make copies of themselves. Some viruses can make us sick, like the ones that cause the flu or the common cold, while others can help scientists learn more about how living things work.

Fungi are another type of microbe that can be helpful or harmful. Some fungi, like the ones that make mushrooms, which are delicious to eat! Others, like the ones that cause athlete's foot or moldy bread, can be annoying or even make us sick.

Protozoa are tiny creatures that live in water and can look like tiny animals under a microscope. Some protozoa are helpful, like the ones that eat bacteria and help keep our water clean. Others can cause diseases like malaria if they get inside our bodies.

Even though they are minimal, microbes are essential to the ecosystem and the health of the Earth. One of their most important jobs is to break down organic waste in the soil, which helps plants grow. As microbes break down organic matter, they release nitrogen, phosphorus, and potassium into the air. Plants then take these nutrients in to help them grow and develop. The decay process brings nutrients back into the soil, making it a good place for new plants to grow.

Also, microbes clean up the world by eliminating pollutants. They are like nature's cleanup crew. Microbes have the amazing ability to break down dangerous chemicals into less dangerous ones anywhere. This includes things like chemical pollution and oil spills. A natural process called bioremediation helps ecosystems get back to a state of balance after human actions have hurt them.

We can learn more about the amazing process of photosynthesis. When we hear this word, we usually think of plants. But some germs, like algae and some bacteria, can make their food in the sun. Microbes make oxygen when they use photosynthesis to turn carbon dioxide and water in the air into carbohydrates. This oxygen is vital for life on Earth because it keeps the weather healthy and gives us air. Simply put, microbes are important for all living things to survive because they keep the amounts of oxygen and carbon dioxide in the air just right.

Believe it or not, you have trillions of microbes in your body right now, and they're helping you stay healthy! These tiny microbes live in your gut and help you digest your food, fight off bad germs, and even make vitamins that keep you strong and healthy.

But sometimes, bad microbes can make us sick. That's why washing your hands often is essential, especially before eating or using the bathroom. And if you get sick, doctors can give you medicine, like antibiotics, to help fight off the bad microbes and make you feel better.

Microbes are crucial for nature and our bodies—they're also used in many everyday things we use and enjoy! For example, did you know that microbes help make some of your favorite foods? They ferment foods like yogurt, cheese, and pickles, giving them their yummy flavors.

Bacteria are tiny but mighty creatures that play a big role in keeping our world healthy and safe. They're not just crucial for nature; they're also accommodating for people like us! Let me explain how.

First, bacteria are like little factories that make medicines to help us when sick. These medicines, called antibiotics, fight off the bad germs that cause infections. It's like sending in a superhero to defeat the bad guys and strengthen our bodies!

But that's not all. Bacteria are also amazing cleaners! Certain bacteria come to the rescue when there's a big mess, like an oil spill in the ocean. They eat up the oil and turn it into more straightforward, less harmful stuff. It's like having tiny janitors who clean up our planet and make it safe for animals to live in again.

So, whether it's fighting off germs or cleaning up pollution, bacteria are like nature's superheroes, working hard behind the scenes to keep us and our planet healthy. The next time you see something small and seemingly unimportant, remember the incredible power of bacteria and how they're making the world a better place for all of us!

Story 3: The Language of Whales

A crew of marine biologists set off on a journey into the ocean's depths, where the waves murmured mysteries, and the wind conveyed tales of faraway lands. This journey took place in the vast expanse of the ocean. Dr. Sarah was one of them. She was a fervent scientist who had a love for the ocean that was as profound as the ocean itself.

Dr. Sarah and her team were eyeing the horizon for any indication of their elusive subjects, the majestic whales, as their research vessel began to cut through the waves. Their eyes were seeking any trace of their animals. Because of their eerie songs, which reverberated through the ocean's depths like a siren's call, these gentle giants of the sea had long been able to captivate people's imagination.

Suddenly, a spout of water emerged from the surface, and not long after that, the sleek and black figure of a humpback whale breached effortlessly into the air. The scientists were overcome with wonder as they entered the scene, and their hearts were excitedly pounding. They had been anticipating this moment for a long time; it was the opportunity to examine these magnificent creatures nearby and discover the factors contributing to their communication.

Dr. Sarah and her team were anxious to catch every element of the whales' behavior and vocalizations, so when they got closer to the whales' pod, they set up their equipment. They put hydrophones into the water and listened closely for the ethereal melodies claimed to emerge from the ocean's depths.

Scientists could see a mysterious sound world develop before their eyes while the hydrophones were submerged in the ocean. They were amazed as they heard the whales' songs echo across the water, filling the ocean with the haunting beauty of their singing.

Every single whale song was a difficult piece of complex patterns of clicks, whistles, and groans. Dr. Sarah was amazed by how deep the noise was, and she knew immediately that it was whale language. This language can share not only knowledge but also feelings and intentions.

Dr. Sarah and her colleagues carefully listened to the records, which helped them figure out how whales talk to each other. The experts found that whales used different calls for different purposes, such as finding their way, hunting, socializing, and courtship.

The finding of "whale dialects" was among the most interesting. These dialects were different ways of talking heard in different pods. Just like people speak different languages and have different accents, whales from different areas have unique languages passed down from generation to generation.

Dr. Sarah and her team spent weeks fully immersing themselves in the captivating world of whales, experiencing wonder, beauty, and mystery. With each passing moment, she propelled them further into the intricate lives of these majestic creatures, driving their eagerness to uncover the secrets hidden beneath the waves.

One of the most remarkable sights they encountered was the mesmerizing courtship displays of the whales. Dr. Sarah and her team observed pods of whales engaging in elaborate rituals to attract potential mates. The males would perform breathtaking acrobatics, leaping out of the water in graceful arcs and emitting hauntingly beautiful songs that echoed across the ocean. These displays were not just a spectacle to behold but also served as a way for the whales to establish dominance and impress potential partners.

But courtship was just one aspect of the whales' social lives. Dr. Sarah was fascinated by the strong bonds that formed within whale pods. These social groups were more than just a collection of individuals—they were tightly knit communities where whales forged deep connections. Through a complex system of calls, clicks, and gestures, the whales communicate with astonishing precision, conveying messages of friendship, cooperation, and even affection.

In one incredible moment, Dr. Sarah witnessed a mother whale caring for her newborn calf, moving her deeply as she observed the whale's depth of emotion. The mother's gentle nudges guided the calf to the surface, teaching it to breathe and navigate the vast ocean waters. This touching display highlighted the bond between parent and child, showcasing maternal instinct and devotion.

Through their observations, Dr. Sarah and her team gained a newfound appreciation for the emotional intelligence of whales. These magnificent creatures exhibited empathy, compassion, and a deep understanding of social dynamics—qualities that resonated with Dr. Sarah on a deeply personal level.

As the sun dipped below the horizon and the whales disappeared into the depths again, Dr. Sarah couldn't help but feel grateful for the opportunity to witness such extraordinary moments. In the whales' language, she had discovered a universal truth—that love, compassion, and connection transcend species boundaries, uniting all living beings in the intricate web of life.

As their research expedition drew close, Dr. Sarah and her team reflected on all they had learned about whale language. They had gained a newfound appreciation for these magnificent creatures and their vital role in the delicate balance of the ocean ecosystem.

But their work was far from over. As they sailed back to shore, Dr. Sarah felt a renewed sense of purpose, knowing that so many mysteries were still waiting to be uncovered beneath the waves. The language of whales was just the beginning—a glimpse into the rich tapestry of life that thrived in the depths of the sea.

Dr. Sarah looked at the vast expanse of water stretching before her as the sun dipped below the horizon, casting a golden glow over the ocean. She knew that the whales' songs would continue to echo through the ages, a timeless melody that spoke to the interconnectedness of all living things and the never-ending power of nature's wonders. And she couldn't wait to dive back in and explore even more of the ocean's mysteries, one discovery at a time.

Experiment: The Transformation of a Butterfly

Welcome, young scientists, to an exciting experiment where we'll witness the incredible transformation of a caterpillar into a beautiful butterfly. Get ready to embark on a journey into the world of metamorphosis and discover the miracle of life firsthand!

Materials Needed:

- A caterpillar (you can find one in your garden or purchase from a pet store or online)

- A clean, spacious container with a lid
- Fresh leaves or plants for the caterpillar to eat
- A magnifying glass
- Notebook and pen to record observations
- Patience and curiosity!

Experiment Steps:

Step 1: Find a Caterpillar

Go on a nature walk in your backyard or a nearby park to look for caterpillars. Look for them on leaves or crawling on the ground. Once you find one, gently pick it up and transfer it to your container.

Step 2: Create a Caterpillar Habitat

Line the bottom of the container with fresh leaves or plants for the caterpillar to eat. Ensure the container has enough ventilation and space for the caterpillar to move around comfortably. Close the lid securely to prevent the caterpillar from escaping.

Step 3: Observe and Feed the Caterpillar

Place the container in a well-lit area where you can easily observe the caterpillar's behavior. Use the magnifying glass to closely examine its features, such as body segments and tiny legs. Offer fresh leaves or plants daily to ensure the caterpillar has enough food.

Step 4: Document the Caterpillar's Growth

Keep a journal to record your observations each day. Note any changes in the caterpillar's size, color, or behavior. Take photos or draw pictures to document its growth and development over time.

Step 5: Watch for Signs of Metamorphosis

As the caterpillar grows, it eventually stops eating and becomes less active. This is a sign that it's preparing to enter the next stage of its life cycle: pupation. Watch for any changes in the caterpillar's appearance or behavior.

Step 6: Witness the Chrysalis Formation

When the caterpillar is ready to pupate, it attaches itself to a surface using silk threads and forms a chrysalis (also known as a cocoon). This process may take several hours, so be patient and observe as the caterpillar transforms before your eyes.

Step 7: Wait for the Butterfly to Emerge

After 10-14 days, the chrysalis will change color, indicating that the butterfly is ready to emerge. Keep a close watch on the chrysalis, as the butterfly will appear soon after. This is an exciting moment that you won't want to miss!

Step 8: Release the Butterfly

Once the butterfly emerges from the chrysalis and its wings fully expand and dry, it's time to release it back into the wild. Take your container outside and open the lid to set the butterfly free. Watch as it takes flight for the first time, a symbol of the miraculous transformation you've witnessed.

You've completed the butterfly transformation experiment! Observing a butterfly's life cycle up close, you've gained a deeper understanding of the miracle of life and the incredible process of metamorphosis. Keep exploring the wonders of nature, and never stop asking questions.

Experiment 2: Exploring the Microscopic World

Today, we are going on an exciting journey to discover the hidden world of microbes. Microbes are tiny living organisms around us, even though we can't see them with our naked eye. They play a crucial role in our world, from helping plants grow to breaking down waste. Prepare to put on your scientist hat and explore this fascinating and mysterious world!

Materials Needed:

- Microscope (if available)
- Glass slides
- Dropper
- Water
- Cotton swabs
- Petri dishes (optional)
- Various items to test (e.g., soil, water, yogurt, fruit, etc.)

Instructions:

Step 1: Set up Your Workstation

Find a clean and quiet area to conduct your experiment. Make sure your microscope is set up correctly and ready to use.

Step 2: Prepare Your Samples

Use a cotton swab to collect samples from different items you want to examine. You can collect samples from soil, water, yogurt, fruits, or anything else interesting. Dip the cotton swab in water and gently rub it on the item's surface to collect microbes.

Step 3: Prepare Slides

Take a glass slide and place a drop of water on it with a dropper. Then, take the cotton swab with the collected sample and gently swirl it in the water drop on the slide. This will transfer the microbes from the sample to the slide.

Step 4: Examine Under the Microscope

Carefully place the prepared slide under the microscope and adjust the focus for a clear view. Look through the eyepiece and start exploring the microscopic world. You may need to adjust the magnification settings to see different details of the microbes.

Step 5: Record Your Observations

As you observe the microbes under the microscope, take notes or draw what you see. Pay attention to the microbes' different shapes, sizes, and movements. If available, you can also take pictures using a smartphone camera attached to the microscope.

Step 6: Experiment with Different Samples

Repeat steps 2-5 with different samples to compare and contrast the microbes from various sources. Try comparing soil microbes with water microbes or yogurt microbes with fruit microbes. See if you can identify any differences or similarities between the samples.

Optional: Grow microbes in Petri dishes—If you can access Petri dishes, you can also try growing microbes from different samples. Place a small amount of each sample on separate Petri dishes and observe how the microbes grow over time. This can be a longer-term experiment to observe microbe diversity and growth.

Safety Tips:

- Always handle the microscope and glass slides carefully to avoid accidents or damage.
- Wash your hands before and after handling samples to prevent contamination.
- Dispose of used cotton swabs and slides properly after the experiment.
- If using Petri dishes, follow proper lab safety protocols and handle them carefully to prevent spills or contamination.

You have explored the hidden world of microbes and learned about these fascinating tiny organisms. Microbes play a vital role in our environment, and studying them helps us better understand their importance. Keep experimenting and exploring the wonders of science!

Chapter Four: The Inventors and Their Inventions

Young innovators, you have opened the door to a new chapter brimming with wonder and discovery! During this journey through the world of inventions, we will investigate the bright minds and groundbreaking discoveries that have contributed to the formation of our world. Throughout history, inventions have propelled humanity forward, opened new opportunities, and significantly changed how we live, work, and play.

What exactly is meant by the term "invention"? Let's say you encounter an issue or challenge that seems impossible. The inventive solution you devise to overcome that obstacle is called an invention. The spark of creativity, the flash of inspiration that changes how we do things and makes our lives simpler, safer, or more joyful, is what we call a "spark of creativity."

This chapter will delve into the stories behind some of the most astonishing inventions throughout history, ranging from ancient marvels to cutting-edge technology. In this lesson, we will study the innovators who dared to dream big, refused to accept the status quo, and persevered in the face of adversity to bring their ideas to life.

On the other hand, inventions are not simply about gadgets and gizmos but about creativity, ingenuity, and finding solutions to problems. They are about taking a new perspective on the world, questioning current affairs, and contemplating ways to improve things. And maybe most significantly, they are about having faith in oneself and one's capacity to make a difference in the world.

Together, we will embark on a voyage through the realm of innovations. During this voyage, we will discover the mysteries of the past, marvel at the marvels of the present, and ponder the possibilities of the future. Who will know? You could be the next great inventor!

Story 1: The Girl Who Played with Water

From a young age, Jessica's inquisitive nature led her to question the world and seek answers to science and nature's mysteries. While her friends frolicked in the fields, Jessica spent her days by the stream, studying the ripple of water and pondering its secrets.

One warm summer's day, as Jessica dipped her toes into the cool, clear waters of the stream, she noticed a change. The once-pristine stream now ran murky, littered with debris and pollutants.

Jessica's heart sank as she realized the pollution's impact on the delicate ecosystem and her village's health.

Driven to make a difference in the world, Jessica embarked on an adventure of research and creativity. She read books and consulted internet resources to learn about water's characteristics and the science behind water filtration. Jessica devised a way to clean up the polluted stream and restore it to its former grandeur. She armed herself with knowledge and dedication.

Jessica's adventure started with her carefully examining the environment around her. With an insatiable appetite for knowledge and a strong need to make a difference, she embarked on a mission to discover the fundamental reason behind the pollution affecting her cherished stream. Jessica used a microscope to thoroughly analyze the water samples collected from various locations along the stream to determine their composition. What she found was disheartening: the waters, which had been clean in the past, were contaminated with a wide variety of contaminants, ranging from hazardous chemicals to debris made of plastic.

Undeterred by the daunting task ahead, Jessica searched for solutions. Drawing inspiration from nature's purification processes, she delved into the intricacies of plant filtration systems and existing water treatment methods. With each discovery, Jessica's determination grew stronger, fueled by the hope of restoring the stream to its former glory.

With a clear vision, Jessica began designing her purification system. Enlisting the help of her parents and neighbors, she gathered materials such as sand, gravel, activated charcoal, and fine mesh screens. Together, they meticulously constructed a prototype filtration device utilizing a large plastic container and layers of filter media.

The heart of Jessica's purification system lay in its simplicity. Contaminated water poured into the top of the container cascaded down through the layers of filter media, each designed to target specific pollutants. The sand and gravel acted as physical barriers, trapping larger particles, while the activated charcoal adsorbed dissolved pollutants and odors, leaving the water purified and clear.

Jessica conducted a series of rigorous experiments to ensure her invention's effectiveness. She measured the turbidity and pH of the water before and after filtration, meticulously documenting any changes. Additionally, she performed tests to detect the presence of harmful bacteria and chemicals, striving for comprehensive results.

The outcome of Jessica's experiments exceeded her expectations. The water's cleanliness significantly decreased, indicating a reduction in suspended particles, while the pH levels stabilized within acceptable ranges. Most importantly, tests for harmful contaminants yielded promising results, confirming the effectiveness of Jessica's filtration system in improving water quality.

But Jessica's journey didn't end there. Encouraged by her success, she continued to refine her invention, exploring ways to make it more accessible and scalable.

At the heart of Jessica's scientific endeavor was the process of hypothesis and experimentation. It all began with a simple question: What was causing the pollution in the stream? Curious and thirsty for knowledge, Jessica hypothesized that the stream's contaminants compromised water quality. She collected water samples and conducted experiments to test her hypothesis, meticulously documenting her findings.

With each experiment, Jessica gained valuable insights into the nature of pollutants and the effectiveness of potential solutions. She learned to refine her methods, adjusting variables and testing different approaches until she achieved the desired results.

Through trial and error, Jessica honed her skills as a scientist, embracing the iterative process of inquiry and discovery.

As Jessica's experiments yielded promising results, she encountered new challenges that required creative problem-solving and perseverance. Whether sourcing materials for her filtration system or interpreting complex data from her experiments, Jessica faced each obstacle with determination and resourcefulness. Through her resilience, she transformed setbacks into opportunities for growth and learning.

Eager to share her invention with her community, Jessica organized a demonstration by the stream. She invited villagers to witness the purification process and taste the clear water from the filtration device. The response was overwhelmingly positive, with villagers expressing gratitude for Jessica's ingenuity and dedication to environmental stewardship.

Word of Jessica's invention spread quickly throughout the village and beyond. Scientists, engineers, and environmentalists praised her innovation and sought to learn from her example. Jessica's passion for science and commitment to protecting the environment made her a local hero, and people celebrated her achievements.

However, for Jessica, the true reward was knowing that her invention had made a tangible difference in the lives of her fellow villagers. With clean, safe water again flowing, the stream became a vibrant ecosystem teeming with life. Fish returned to its waters, birds sang in the trees, and the village flourished again.

As Jessica reflected on her journey, she realized the power of science and innovation to effect positive change in the world. She hoped that her story would inspire others to dream big, to question the status quo, and to harness their curiosity and creativity to make a difference.

And so, as you embark on your journey of discovery, remember Jessica's example. Dare to dream, dare to explore, and dare to make a difference. For in the hands of a curious mind, even the slightest idea can spark a revolution and change the world for the better.

Story 2: The Code Breakers

In the not-so-distant past, inventors and scientists dared to dream of a world where machines could think, calculate, and solve complex problems. These pioneers, known as the Code Breakers, embarked on a journey of innovation and discovery that would forever change the course of history.

Imagine a young boy named Alan Turing growing up in England in the early 1900s. Alan was unlike other children—he had a remarkable gift for numbers and puzzles. From a young age, he was fascinated by the mysteries of mathematics and logic, spending hours solving complex equations and unraveling tricky riddles.

On the other hand, Alan's journey was difficult. He was subjected to discrimination and prejudice because he had a distinctive style of thinking in a society that frequently looked down upon people who were different. Despite his difficulties, he stayed resolute in pursuing his goal: to discover the mysteries of the cosmos by applying mathematics and logic.

Alan's abilities drew the attention of British intelligence organizations just as the clouds of World War II began to gather over Europe. Enigma was a complex encryption machine used by the German military to send coded messages. This made it extremely difficult for the Allied forces to decrypt the German military's signals. It was impossible to decipher the Enigma code, which was similar to a puzzle with an infinite number of possible possibilities.

But Alan was not one to shy away from a challenge. Alongside a team of fellow Bletchley Park code-breakers, Alan tackled the Enigma code head-on. They worked tirelessly, pouring over intercepted messages and analyzing patterns in the code. It was like trying to solve the world's most complicated crossword puzzle, with stakes higher than anyone could imagine.

After months of painstaking work, Alan had a breakthrough. He devised a groundbreaking machine called the Bombe—a complex contraption that could rapidly test combinations of Enigma settings and decipher messages in record time. The Bombe was like a supercharged calculator, crunching numbers at lightning speed to unlock the secrets hidden within the Enigma code.

With the help of the Bombe, Alan and his team broke the Enigma code and gained access to vital intelligence that helped turn the tide of the war. Their work was nothing short of miraculous, saving countless lives and helping to end one of the darkest chapters in human history.

Alan Turing's contributions to cryptography and computing were nothing short of revolutionary. His work laid the foundation for modern computing and artificial intelligence, shaping human history in ways still felt today.

Despite adversity and discrimination, Alan Turing never lost his passion for mathematics and logic. His perseverance and determination inspire us all, reminding us that anything is possible with creativity, courage, and a little ingenuity.

The Bombe's success marked a turning point in the war effort, providing invaluable intelligence that helped Allied forces thwart enemy attacks and turn the tide of battle in their favor. Turing's contributions to cryptography and computing earned him a place in history as one of the greatest minds of the 20th century.

Imagine yourself in New York City in the early 1900s, a bustling metropolis filled with towering skyscrapers and bustling streets. Here, a young girl named Grace Hopper was born, destined to defy societal norms and blaze a trail in mathematics and technology.

Grace was no ordinary girl. Her passion for numbers and knack for solving puzzles set her apart from her peers. While other girls dreamed of becoming teachers or nurses, Grace dreamed of unraveling the mysteries of the universe through mathematics and logic.

Despite opposition and skepticism from those around her, Grace remained undeterred in her pursuit of knowledge. She devoured books on mathematics and science, soaking up every piece of information like a sponge. Her thirst for learning was insatiable, driving her to excel in her studies and pursue a career in a field dominated by men.

Grace dared to dream of a different future in a society where women expected her to stay home and raise children. She enrolled at Vassar College, where she studied mathematics and graduated with top honors. But Grace's journey was just beginning—she knew that if she wanted to make a real impact in the world, she would need to push herself even further.

After earning her Ph.D. in mathematics from Yale University, Grace set her sights on a new challenge: joining the U.S. Navy Reserves during World War II. Despite facing skepticism and resistance from male colleagues who believed that women had no place in the military, Grace proved herself to be a capable and dedicated officer.

During her time in the Navy, Grace's talents caught the attention of her superiors, who recognized her keen analytical skills and problem-solving abilities. They assigned her to work on a top-secret project at Harvard University that would change the course of history forever.

Alongside a team of engineers and scientists, Grace embarked on a mission to build the world's first programmable digital computer—the Mark I. This massive electromechanical machine was unlike anything the world had ever seen, capable of performing complex calculations and solving mathematical equations with unprecedented speed and accuracy.

For years, Grace and her team labored tirelessly, working day and night to design and build the Mark I. They encountered countless obstacles and setbacks, but Grace refused to give up. Her determination and perseverance were unwavering, driving her to overcome every challenge.

Finally, after years of hard work, they completed the Mark I—a towering monument to human ingenuity and innovation. Its completion marked a significant milestone in computing history, paving the way for developing more advanced and sophisticated machines in the decades to come.

Grace's pioneering work in computer science earned her numerous accolades and honors, including the Presidential Medal of Freedom, the highest civilian award in the United States. But her greatest legacy is the inspiration she has provided to future generations of inventors, scientists, and innovators.

The legacy of Grace Hopper and the Code Breakers lives on, inspiring countless individuals to push the boundaries of what is possible and strive for greatness. Their creativity, perseverance, and problem-solving skills have forever changed the world, leaving behind a legacy of innovation and discovery that will shape human history for generations.

Story 3: The Light of Edison

In the center of the crowded streets of 19th-century America, unstoppable curiosity and a vision to change the world overpowered young Tom Edison. This voyage into the realm of invention and discovery would eventually lead to one of the most influential inventions in history—the electric light bulb. This is the tale of Edison's relentless inventions and goal to enlighten the planet.

The curiosity and the desire to learn were the main features of young Thomas Edison's childhood. Growing up in Milan, Ohio, he always had a knack for fixing things and doing science experiments in his homemade lab. One day, while working as a telegraph operator, Edison saw that the wires overheated and started to spark because there was too much electricity. This saw the birth of the idea that he later tested with electric lightning.

Like many other people who worked with electricity, Edison became increasingly interested in making a reliable and inexpensive source of manufactured light. Candles, oil lamps, and gas lights were the only ways people could light up rooms at the time. However, none of them were very bright, and all of them put their safety at great risk. Oil lamps and candles started many fires, and gas lights emitted poisonous fumes that were bad for your health.

Before building the light bulb, Thomas Edison had to learn about electric currents and the different kinds of materials that could be used as filaments. He researched and tried many carbonized materials, such as cotton thread and bamboo. Even though Edison had many setbacks and failures in his work, each one brought him closer to his goals.

Even though Edison had conducted thousands of tests before 1879, he finally made a significant discovery that year. He discovered that a carbonized bamboo thread could glow for a long time if placed inside a glass bulb and kept away from the air. During this time, Edison created the first electric light bulb that businesses could use.

Thomas Edison changed the world of electricity in many ways, not just by making the light bulb. Early on, he realized there needed to be a safe and efficient way to create and distribute electricity so everyone could use electric light. Because of this, he became one of the first people to use direct current (DC) electricity, causing a massive change in how towns receive power.

Edison made a big step forward in the field of electricity when he opened the first electric power station in New York City in 1882. This power station was a groundbreaking project located in lower Manhattan. It gave power to nearby homes, businesses, and lighting. Cities all over the United States started getting electricity, which changed how people lived and worked. It was the start of a new era.

Though Edison was a leader in DC electricity, he became rivals with other famous thinkers and engineers, especially Nikola Tesla and George Westinghouse. The "War of Currents" started as a heated argument over whether direct current (DC) or alternating current (AC) was better for general use.

Edison pushed for DC energy because he thought it was safer and easier to work with than AC. He set up a network of DC power stations and pushed for towns nationwide to use them. On the other hand, Tesla and Westinghouse argued in favor of AC energy, saying that it could send power over longer distances with less loss and work with more efficient electric motors.

Proponents of DC and AC became increasingly competitive, and their fight became very public. Both sides used aggressive advertising and public demos to showcase their systems' best features. Edison even shocked animals, showing that AC wasn't safe. This eventually backfired and hurt his image.

Even though there was much competition and debate during the "War of Currents," Edison's reputation as a leading inventor and innovator stayed the same. He made important advances in electricity and technology that made our world possible. The building of electric power plants, the development of reliable electric grids, and the general use of electric lighting changed society and enabled progress in many fields.

Edison's impact exceeded his inventions and included his thoughts on new ideas and business. He believed trying new things and failing were essential to the invention process. He famously said, "I have not failed." I just thought of 10,000 ways that this won't work. This attitude of toughness and persistence continues to motivate creators, scientists, and businesspeople worldwide.

One of Edison's lesser-known but equally important inventions was the phonograph, which recorded and played back sound. This groundbreaking invention revolutionized the music industry and paved the way for modern recording and playback device development.

The story of Thomas Edison and the invention of the electric light bulb is a testament to the power of curiosity, creativity, and perseverance. Edison's journey from a curious kid tinkering with gadgets to a renowned inventor and innovator serves as a reminder that anyone can change the world with determination and a willingness to push the boundaries of what is possible. So, the next time you flip a light switch or listen to music, remember the incredible journey that led to these everyday conveniences and the brilliant mind of Thomas Edison that made it all possible.

Experiment 1: The Journey of Invention

In this exciting experiment, we will embark on a journey of invention, exploring the creative process and problem-solving skills that inventors use to develop new ideas and technologies. Get ready to unleash your imagination and curiosity as we dive into the world of innovation!

Materials Needed:

- Paper and pencils
- Various household items (e.g., cardboard, tape, rubber bands, straws, etc.)
- Scissors
- Markers or crayons
- Optional: Craft supplies like glue, construction paper, and pipe cleaners

Experiment Steps:

Step 1: Brainstorming Ideas (30 minutes)

- Gather all the materials needed for the experiment.
- Sit down in a comfortable and quiet space where you can focus.
- Start by brainstorming ideas for inventions. Think about everyday problems or challenges and how to solve them with a new invention.

- Write down your ideas on a piece of paper. Be creative and think outside the box!

Step 2: Designing Your Invention (30 minutes)

- Choose one of your brainstormed ideas to develop into an invention.

- Sketch a detailed design of your invention on another piece of paper. Include labels and descriptions of how it works.

- Use the household items and craft supplies to prototype your invention. Feel free to experiment with different materials and designs until you're satisfied with your prototype.

Step 3: Testing and Refining (30 minutes)

- Once you've built your prototype, it's time to test it out!

- Identify a problem or challenge that your invention solves. For example, if your invention is a new type of backpack, test its durability and storage capacity.

- Conduct tests and experiments to see how well your invention works. Make observations and take notes on any improvements or modifications needed.

Step 4: Presenting Your Invention (30 minutes)

- Prepare a presentation to showcase your invention to others.

- Create a poster or slideshow with pictures and descriptions of your invention, including how it works and its potential benefits.

- Practice your presentation and be ready to answer questions from your audience.

Step 5: Reflection and Feedback (15 minutes)

- Reflect on your journey of invention. What did you learn during the process? What challenges did you encounter, and how did you overcome them?

- Share your invention with friends, family, or classmates and ask for their feedback. What do they think of it? Are there any suggestions for improvement?

You've completed the journey of invention and explored the exciting world of creativity, problem-solving, and innovation. Remember, the sky's the limit when it comes to inventing, so keep exploring, experimenting, and dreaming up new ideas. Who knows, you might just invent the next big thing!

Experiment 2:

In this experiment, we will jump into the fascinating world of electricity and learn about its properties and behavior. Get ready to conduct exciting experiments and discover the power of electricity firsthand!

Materials Needed:

- Battery (AA or AAA)
- Light bulb (LED works best for safety)
- Electrical wires with alligator clips
- Safety goggles
- Optional: Voltmeter or multimeter for measuring voltage

Experiment Steps:

Step 1: Safety First (5 minutes)

- Put on your safety goggles to protect your eyes during the experiment.

- Make sure to work in a clean and uncluttered area to avoid accidents.

Step 2: Understanding Electricity (10 minutes)

- Gather around and discuss what electricity is with your young scientists. Explain that electricity is the flow of electric charge through conductive materials.

- Show them the battery and explain that it provides the energy needed to create electricity.

Step 3: Assembling the Circuit (15 minutes)

- Take the battery, light bulb, and electrical wires with alligator clips.

- Attach one end of the wire to the battery's positive terminal (+) using the alligator clip.

- Attach the other end of the wire to the light bulb's base.

- Attach a second wire from the tip of the light bulb to the negative terminal (-) of the battery.

Step 4: Testing the Circuit (10 minutes)

- Double-check that all connections are secure and there are no loose wires.

- Hold the light bulb away from the battery and ask the kids what they think will happen when you connect the wires to the battery terminals.

- Connect the wires to the battery terminals and observe what happens. The light bulb should light up, indicating electricity flowing through the circuit.

Step 5: Exploring Conductors and Insulators (15 minutes)

- Discuss the concepts of conductors and insulators with the kids. Explain that conductors allow electricity to flow through them easily, while insulators block or limit the flow of electricity.

- Test different materials to see if they are conductors or insulators. Use metal objects (conductors) and plastic objects (insulators).

- Have the kids predict whether each material will allow electricity to flow through the circuit. Test each material by replacing the wire with the material and observing if the light bulb lights up.

Step 6: Measuring Voltage (15 minutes)

- For older kids or those interested in more advanced experiments, introduce the concept of voltage and its relationship to electricity.

- A voltmeter or multimeter measures the voltage across the battery terminals. Explain that voltage is the force that pushes electric charge through a circuit.

- Have the kids record the voltage readings and discuss how changing the number of batteries or their arrangement affects the voltage.

Step 7: Troubleshooting and Experimentation (15 minutes)

- Encourage the kids to experiment with the circuit by making changes, such as adding more batteries, using different light bulbs, or rearranging the wires.

- Ask them to predict what will happen before making changes and observe the outcomes. Encourage them to troubleshoot if the light bulb doesn't appear as expected.

Step 8: Discussion and Conclusion (10 minutes)

- Gather the kids to discuss what they learned during the experiment.

- Recap the fundamental concepts of electricity, conductors, insulators, and voltage.

- Ask open-ended questions to stimulate critical thinking, such as "What other experiments could we do to learn more about electricity?" or "How is electricity used in our daily lives?"

Well done, young explorers! You've delved into the fascinating world of electricity and conducted thrilling experiments to unravel its mysteries. Keep up the exploration and experimentation with electricity. Who knows? You might be on the brink of inventing the next groundbreaking electrical marvel!

Chapter Five: The Power of Energy

Welcome to a world where the incredible power of energy is right before our eyes! Have you ever wondered how sunlight can turn into electricity or how a light breeze can power whole cities? This chapter takes us on an exciting adventure through the amazing world of energy. We'll learn about the excellent benefits of solar power, wind power, and the amazing possibilities of fusion.

Think about a world where the sun's warm and welcoming rays are the key to powering schools, homes, and whole neighborhoods. That's how solar power works! Solar panels can take in the energy from the sun and turn it into electricity. This gives us access to a clean and green source of power. But how does everything work? What happens when sunlight hits the solar cells? How does that energy become power that we can use?

Let's look at the dancing winds that whisper through the sky. Have you ever marveled at the strength of the wind and wondered what else people use it for besides raising kites and moving leaves? Wind power is an exciting option! With their tall blades, giant windmills turn the wind's kinetic energy into electricity. But how do these turbines use the wind's energy to make electricity? What happens inside those moving blades?

There's more, though! Thanks to the fantastic power of fusion, our journey into the heart of the stars is about to begin. Have you ever looked at the stars at night and wondered how the sun and other stars get their power?

Fusion, the process that makes the sun work, is the key to creating almost endless energy. By pressing and heating atoms together very quickly, we can release a tremendous amount of energy, much more than what's possible with regular sources. How do scientists make these harsh conditions happen here on Earth? What are the pros and cons of using fusion power to meet our energy needs?

Come with us on this exciting journey into the world of energy, where we will meet people interested in discovering more and where the mysteries of the universe will come to life right before our eyes. Let's find out how to use solar power, control the wind's endless energy, and explore the fiery worlds of fusion to see the fantastic possibilities that energy has for our world!

Story 1: The Sun's Gift

In the bustling city where these curious children lived, they noticed something that bothered them deeply—the thick layer of smog and pollution hanging over their streets. They wondered if there was a better way to power their city without harming the environment. That's when they stumbled upon the fascinating world of solar energy.

Their journey into solar energy began with a thirst for knowledge. They wanted to understand how sunlight, something so abundant and freely available, could be transformed into electricity. So, they delved into books, attended workshops, and consulted with experts to unravel the science behind solar power.

What they discovered was truly remarkable. Solar power relies on photovoltaic (PV) cells, which are the building blocks of solar panels. These cells are made from special materials like silicon and have a unique property—when sunlight hits them, they release electrons. This release of electrons creates an electric current, which can then be harnessed and used as electricity.

The children were fascinated by this process. They discovered that solar panels consist of many connected PV cells. When sunlight falls on these panels, each cell contributes its share of electric current, generating usable electricity. This electricity can power homes, schools, businesses, and even entire cities!

After grasping the basics of solar energy, the curious children were eager to witness its magic firsthand. They longed to see sunlight transform into electricity right before their eyes, so they embarked on an exciting project to build a small solar panel system.

First, they gathered all the necessary materials: photovoltaic (PV) cells, wires, a charge controller, and a battery. These components were crucial in creating a functional solar panel setup. With the help of their mentors and guides, they learned how to assemble these components step by step.

The PV cells were the heart of their solar panel. Manufacturers made these cells from unique materials like silicon, which could generate electricity when exposed to sunlight. The wires served as the pathways for the electric current to flow, connecting the PV cells to the charge controller and battery. The charge controller acted as a regulator, ensuring the battery received the right amount of electricity without getting overcharged. Finally, the battery stores the excess energy generated by the solar panel during sunny hours, which can be used later when sunlight isn't available.

Once they assembled their solar panel, they carefully placed it in an area where it could receive plenty of sunlight throughout the day. They positioned it facing the sun, maximizing its exposure to its rays. Then, they eagerly waited for the sun to work its magic.

As the sun's rays hit the solar panel, something incredible happened. The PV cells in the panel absorbed the sunlight and started generating electricity. This electric current flowed through the wires, reaching the charge controller and battery. The charge controller efficiently managed the flow of electricity, ensuring that the battery received just the right amount to charge without any damage.

The children watched in amazement as their solar panel setup came to life. They could see the electric current flowing through the wires, charging the battery, and storing the energy. To test their creation, they connected small devices like lights and fans to the battery. And just like that, the stored solar energy powered these devices, illuminating the lights and spinning the fans.

Their experiment was a success, and they were thrilled to witness the magic of solar energy in action. They experienced firsthand how to harness sunlight to generate clean and renewable electricity. This hands-on experience deepened their understanding of solar energy and sparked their passion for renewable technologies and sustainability.

Their experiment taught them valuable lessons about the power of renewable energy. They realized solar energy is clean, sustainable, versatile, and accessible. With solar panels, anyone can tap into the sun's abundant energy and reduce their reliance on fossil fuels, which contribute to pollution and climate change.

The children's journey into solar energy didn't end with a simple experiment. It sparked a passion for sustainability and innovation in their community. They shared their knowledge with others, encouraging them to consider solar energy a viable alternative to traditional power sources. They organized workshops, demonstrations, and awareness campaigns to spread the word about solar power's benefits.

Excited by their newfound understanding, the children set their sights on creating a solar-powered system for their city. They knew solar panels, also known as solar modules, were the key to capturing sunlight and generating electricity. Each panel consisted of multiple PV cells connected in series and parallel to produce the desired voltage and current.

It was crucial to select the right location for their solar installation. They scouted rooftops, parks, and open spaces to find the perfect spot with maximum sunlight exposure throughout the day. After careful consideration, they chose a rooftop in the city center, ensuring unobstructed access to sunlight and minimal shading from surrounding buildings.

With their location secured, the children embarked on the process of installing solar panels. They worked with experienced technicians and engineers to mount the panels securely, orienting them to face the sun's path for optimal energy production. They carefully laid out wiring and connections to ensure efficiency and safety.

The PV cells worked magic as the panels absorbed sunlight, converting photons into electrons and generating DC (direct current) electricity. But the journey didn't end there. The children understood that converting DC electricity into AC (alternating current) is necessary for its use in homes and businesses. They installed inverters, devices that transformed DC electricity into AC, making it compatible with the city's electrical grid.

The part of their solar project that involved monitoring and care was essential for ensuring their solar-powered system worked well and efficiently. To do this, the kids set up high-tech monitoring systems for energy production, system performance, and general efficiency.

One of the most important parts of their monitoring system was a data logger linked to the solar cells and inverters. This data logger tracked important numbers like temperature, voltage, current, power flow, and solar irradiance (how much sunlight hit the panels). By collecting this information daily, the kids learned how their solar panels worked in different weather conditions and times of the day.

The kids used cloud-based software systems that provided detailed analytics reporting tools and real-time monitoring. These platforms allowed them to see the data the data logger had received, analyze trends over time, and identify any problems or oddities that required fixing. For instance, they could tell if a specific solar screen wasn't working well or if shading problems were stopping energy production.

The kids learned how to read their tracking systems' information and use it to make smart choices about improving their solar-powered system. They could change the tilt angle or orientation of the solar panels to get the most sunlight. If there were any technical problems, they could quickly fix them and plan regular maintenance to ensure the system lasts as long as possible.

The kids analyzed how their solar project would impact the environment and discovered its potential to bring significant positive changes. They thought lowering greenhouse gas emissions would be one of the most important effects. Using solar energy instead of fossil fuels to create power keeps harmful gases like carbon dioxide, methane, and nitrous oxide from entering the air. These changes lessened the greenhouse effect and slowed climate change and world warming.

The fact that they used solar energy also helped protect natural resources. Unlike fossil fuels, which cannot be replenished repeatedly, people can utilize sunlight as a plentiful and renewable resource without depleting natural supplies. By using solar power, the kids reduced their use of and mining fossil fuels, protecting essential resources for future generations.

Another essential benefit they saw was the better quality of the air. Traditional energy sources like coal and oil-based power plants release pollutants like sulfur dioxide, nitrogen oxides, and particulate matter, which dirty the air and cause lung health problems. They helped clean the air and make the world healthier for themselves and their community by switching to clean solar energy.

These environmental discoveries shocked the kids, making them want to do more than work on their solar project. They became strong supporters of green energy and environmental protection. They told others about the benefits of solar power and urged others to follow suit. They thought their work would start a larger movement toward a better, cleaner, and more stable future for everyone on Earth.

Their solar-powered system wasn't just about generating electricity; it was about inspiring change and fostering a culture of sustainability. The children organized community events, workshops, and educational programs to share their knowledge and experiences with others. They collaborated with local schools, businesses, and government agencies to promote solar energy adoption and advocate for policy changes that supported renewable energy initiatives.

The impact of their solar project extended beyond their city and across the region. They connected with other young innovators and environmental activists worldwide, forming a global network of solar enthusiasts committed to creating a brighter, cleaner future for all.

As the sun set on their journey into solar energy, the children reflected on the lessons they had learned and the impact they had made. They realized that the sun's power was not just about generating electricity but about empowerment, innovation, and resilience. They had tapped into a boundless energy source that could light up their city and ignite a passion for sustainability in future generations.

Their journey was a testament to the transformative power of young minds, determination, and renewable energy. As they looked toward the horizon, they saw a world powered by the sun, where clean energy was the norm, and every ray of sunlight was a step closer to a brighter tomorrow. And so, their story continued, a shining example of the endless possibilities of harnessing the sun's power.

Story 2: The Wind that Powers the Future

The kids' trip into the world of wind energy was exciting and full of new things they learned. They started their quest for information by reading books, attending workshops, and asking experts for help. They understood that wind energy originates from moving air masses in the Earth's atmosphere and can be utilized repeatedly. This movement is known as wind, possessing kinetic energy that can generate power in wind turbines.

The first thing they learned was how wind machines work. They found that a wind turbine has several essential parts, such as blades, a rotor, a gearbox, an engine, and a tower. Engineers built it so the blades can spin by capturing the wind's kinetic energy. The blades are attached to a gearbox that speeds up the rotation. Once the high-speed rotor hits a generator, mechanical energy becomes electricity that can power homes, schools, and businesses.

As they learned more about the science behind wind energy, the kids learned about the things that affect how much energy a wind machine can make. They found that the wind speed, the blades' size, the tower's height, and the turbine's location are all significant in determining how well it works. They also learned about wind models and how meteorologists use them to determine where wind farms work best and predict how the wind will blow.

One of the most exciting things about their research was learning how windmills can work with nature. They realized that before building wind farms, experts conducted an environmental impact assessment to ensure they would have the least possible effect on ecosystems, wildlife, and nearby towns. They also learned that modern wind turbines are designed to be bird-friendly, with slower blade speeds and clever sensors that can detect when birds are approaching and adjust how the turbine operates to avoid collisions with them.

The kids investigated grid integration as well. They learned how to integrate electricity generated from wind farms into the power grid for people to use. They also understood that wind energy could be stored in batteries or combined with other green energy sources, such as solar power, to create a more reliable and long-lasting energy system.

Due to their natural curiosity and sense of wonder, the kids were interested in using the wind to make electricity. They first became interested in wind energy because they wanted to learn more about it.

Mentors and guides helped them along the way; they knew a lot about the subjects and could give them good advice. The teachers said wind turbines, also called windmills, were the best way to use wind power. The turbines are tall poles with big blades connected to a rotor. When the wind blew, the blades turned, which turned the rotor, which was linked to a generator and made electricity.

The kids were so interested in this idea that they made their small wind machine. With the help of their teachers, they got things like

PVC pipes, wooden boards, plastic blades, and a small engine. They carefully combined these parts to make a small wind machine that worked, just like the ones they had read about and seen on TV.

Once the kids had finished building their wind machine, they set it up in an open field with a steady wind flow while their adults watched over them. They were very interested in seeing how the wind caught the turbine's blades and made them spin elegantly. The rotor hooked up to the generator turned on, making a little power that lit up a small bulb on the turbine. The kids cheered joyfully as they saw how the wind could produce electricity.

After their test went well, the children's goals went through the roof. They wanted to build a community wind farm to give their town clean, long-lasting power. They understood that such a big project would require the assistance of people who plan and construct giant wind turbines.

The kids took on the massive project of building their wind farm with the help of their town and the local government. They looked at many places, like open areas and the tops of hills, to find places with strong, consistent winds that would be good for putting up wind turbines. After much thought and planning, they chose a spot on the edge of town where the wind would blow steadily all year.

The windmills were designed and built as the next part of their project. The kids worked very hard to create the turbines' blades, rotors, towers, and other parts while supervised by experienced engineers and technicians. They learned about aerodynamics, blade design, and structural engineering to ensure their windmills worked well and were safe.

As the kids worked on building the wind farm, they encountered many problems and hurdles. They needed help getting materials, keeping track of procedures, and coordinating the work of several teams. However, they stayed focused on creating a sustainable energy source for their town and the environment, thanks to the unwavering support of their teachers and the community.

Their hard work and determination led to the successful completion of the community wind farm. Adults taught them, and the wind turbines stood tall and proud, using the wind's power to make clean, long-lasting energy for the town. The kids made their dreams come true, showing how powerful young minds can be and how renewable energy options can help the environment.

The kids, their mentors, and people in the neighborhood worked together to make their wind farm project successful. Together, they showed how natural energy sources like wind power can help make the future greener and more stable for future generations.

Finally, after months of hard work and dedication, the wind farm was complete. The children stood in awe as they looked at the towering turbines, their blades poised to capture the wind's energy. The turbines are connected to a power grid, enabling the distribution of the generated electricity to homes, schools, and businesses in their town.

As the wind blew and the turbines spun gracefully, the children marveled at the power of nature and human ingenuity. They witnessed the turbines generating clean and renewable electricity, reducing the town's reliance on fossil fuels and lowering carbon emissions. They knew that their wind farm was about generating electricity, positively impacting the environment, and inspiring others to embrace renewable energy solutions.

The children organized community events, workshops, and educational programs to share their knowledge and experiences with others. They invited people from neighboring towns and cities to visit their wind farms, learn about wind energy, and explore ways to adopt renewable energy practices in their own lives.

Their wind farm symbolizes hope and progress, a testament to the power of teamwork, innovation, and sustainability. It inspired other communities to follow suit and embark on renewable energy projects. The children's dream of harnessing the wind's power had become a reality, transforming their town into a beacon of clean energy and environmental stewardship.

The children felt fulfilled and proud as the sun set on their journey into wind energy. They knew that they had made a difference—not just for their community but for the planet as a whole. Their story was a shining example of renewable energy's endless possibilities and the transformative impact it could have on the world. And so, their journey continued as a testament to young minds' boundless potential and the wind's enduring power.

Story 3: The Quest for Fusion

In the vast universe, stars shine brightly because they undergo nuclear fusion. This process happens when tiny particles inside stars, called atoms, come together to form new elements, like helium while releasing a lot of energy.

Here on Earth, scientists are trying to recreate this process in a controlled way to produce energy. They use special devices called fusion reactors that heat atoms to very high temperatures and squeeze them together. When this happens, the atoms fuse, creating new elements and releasing much energy.

The fantastic thing about nuclear fusion is that it's a clean and almost limitless energy source. It doesn't produce harmful pollution like some other energy sources, and the fuel it uses is abundant in nature.

If scientists can figure out how to make fusion reactors work on a large scale, we could have a new way to generate electricity without harming the environment. It would be like bringing a piece of the sun's power to Earth!

In a future not so far away, where scientific progress and technological marvels coexist with natural wonders, a group of passionate scientists embarked on an awe-inspiring quest—one that could change the course of human history. Led by Dr. Elena Chen, a brilliant physicist with a vision of sustainable energy, this diverse team of experts delved deep into the realms of nuclear fusion, a process that powers the stars and holds the key to unlocking virtually limitless energy here on Earth.

Their journey began in a sprawling research facility amidst rolling hills and tranquil lakes. Dr. Chen, known for her boundless curiosity and innovative thinking, gathered a team of scientists, engineers, and technicians from around the globe. Each member brought unique skills, perspectives, and expertise, forming a powerhouse of knowledge and creativity.

The quest for fusion energy was not merely a scientific endeavor but a grand adventure that would test the limits of human understanding and technological prowess. Fusion, which fuels the sun and other stars, involves merging light atomic nuclei to release tremendous energy. The challenge lay in replicating this process on Earth in a controlled and sustainable manner.

The team utilized cutting-edge technology and groundbreaking theories to achieve this monumental task. At the heart of their efforts was the creation of a fusion reactor—a colossal structure that would mimic the extreme conditions found in stars' cores. Here, temperatures soared to millions of degrees Celsius, and pressures reached staggering levels, creating an environment ripe for nuclear fusion.

Led by the enthusiastic Dr. Elena Chen, these scientists were on a quest to harness the incredible power of high-powered lasers and magnetic fields to create something extraordinary—plasma.

Now, what exactly is a plasma? Well, imagine a superheated gas filled with electrically charged particles. That's what a plasma is! Scientists need it as the fuel for fusion reactions.

To create this plasma, they used powerful lasers and magnetic fields. The lasers were like beams of concentrated light that could heat things really, really hot. And the magnetic fields were like invisible forces that could control and shape the plasma.

Something incredible happened when the scientists fired up the lasers and activated the magnetic fields. The plasma began forming and filled with hydrogen isotopes—tiny particles resembling the building blocks of atoms. As the lasers and magnetic fields converged, they compressed and heated the plasma, making it hotter and denser.

And then, magic! Well, not real magic, but something pretty close. The super-hot plasma and the hydrogen isotopes started colliding and fusing like stars creating energy in space. This fusion process released bursts of energy—a lot of it! This energy was like a burst of light and heat, precisely what the scientists hoped for.

This was the first step in their journey, but it was crucial. It showed them they could create and control plasma using lasers and magnetic fields, a big deal in nuclear fusion. It was like unlocking a door to a whole new realm of possibilities for clean and sustainable energy.

Dr. Chen and her team were familiar with the challenges. As they delved deeper into their quest for harnessing the power of nuclear fusion, they encountered numerous hurdles that tested their skills and creativity. One of their biggest challenges was designing and constructing advanced plasma containment systems. When dealing with something as hot and energetic as a fusion reaction, you must ensure that the plasma, the superheated gas that fuels the fusion, doesn't escape and cause havoc.

To address this challenge, the team devised ingenious solutions. They designed specialized containment chambers lined with high-tech materials to withstand the intense heat and pressure generated during fusion. These chambers were like strongholds, keeping the plasma tightly confined and allowing the scientists to control and manipulate it.

But containment was just one part of the puzzle. The team also needed to closely monitor and study the plasma's behavior to ensure stability and control. This meant developing sophisticated diagnostics and monitoring devices that could penetrate the fusion process's heart. They created sensors and detectors to measure temperature, pressure, and energy levels inside the containment chambers, providing valuable data that guided their experiments and adjustments.

However, the real game-changer came with magnetic confinement. Imagine giant, powerful magnets surrounding the plasma, like invisible hands holding it in place. These magnets were the key to achieving a significant breakthrough—the sustained fusion reactions. By confining and manipulating the plasma using magnetic fields, the team achieved something remarkable: they kept the fusion reactions going for extended periods, generating steady energy.

This breakthrough marked a significant leap forward in their quest for fusion power. It showed that their containment systems and monitoring devices were working effectively, and it opened up new possibilities for exploring fusion as a clean and virtually limitless energy source. The team celebrated this milestone but knew that more challenges and discoveries were waiting on the horizon as they continued their journey into the fascinating world of nuclear fusion.

But the journey was far from over. The team continued to refine their techniques, optimize their reactor designs, and explore novel approaches to enhancing fusion efficiency. They also delved into the intricacies of plasma physics, studying the dynamics of particle interactions, energy transfer mechanisms, and confinement strategies.

One of the most promising avenues they pursued was magnetic confinement fusion, specifically tokamak reactors. These doughnut-shaped devices used magnetic fields to trap and control the plasma, allowing for sustained fusion reactions. To achieve optimal performance, the team tirelessly experimented with different plasma configurations, magnetic field strengths, and reactor geometries.

As their research progressed, they made groundbreaking discoveries about plasma behavior, fusion instabilities, and energy output. They developed innovative materials capable of withstanding the extreme conditions inside a fusion reactor, paving the way for safer and more reliable fusion power plants.

But fusion was not without its challenges. The team grappled with plasma instabilities, energy loss mechanisms, and reactor maintenance issues. They worked tirelessly to address these challenges, collaborating with experts from various disciplines and drawing inspiration from nature's fusion reactors—the stars.

One of the team's proudest moments was achieving sustained fusion, in which the energy produced by fusion reactions exceeded the energy input required to maintain the process. This breakthrough demonstrated the feasibility and potential of fusion energy as a clean, safe, and virtually limitless power source.

However, fusion energy's impact extended far beyond the confines of the research facility. Dr. Chen and her team envisioned a world powered by fusion—where energy was abundant, affordable, and environmentally friendly. They saw fusion as a solution to pressing global challenges such as climate change, energy security, and resource depletion.

As news of their achievements spread, the world took notice. Governments, industries, and communities rallied behind the vision of fusion energy, investing in research, development, and infrastructure. Fusion power plants emerged, heralding a new clean and sustainable energy production era.

But perhaps fusion energy's most profound impact was its potential to transform lives. Fusion provided a lifeline in remote areas without access to traditional power sources, bringing light, heat, and opportunity to communities worldwide. It powered cities, industries, and transportation systems, driving economic growth and social progress.

As the years passed, Dr. Chen and her team continued to push the boundaries of fusion technology. They explored advanced fusion concepts, such as inertial confinement and magnetic target fusion, aiming to unlock even greater efficiencies and energy outputs.

Their journey was not without its setbacks and challenges. Their experiments faced funding constraints, technical hurdles, and occasional setbacks. But through perseverance, collaboration, and unwavering determination, they overcame each obstacle, inching closer to their ultimate goal: a world powered by fusion energy.

Today, fusion energy proves human ingenuity, innovation, and the power of collective effort. It is a ray of hope for a sustainable future where clean energy is abundant, accessible, and equitable for all. As Dr. Chen and her team reflect on their journey, they see the culmination of scientific achievement and the dawn of a new era fueled by the fusion of science, imagination, and possibility.

Experiment 1: Exploring Solar Energy

Solar energy is a powerful and renewable source of energy that comes from the sun. In this experiment, we will explore how solar energy works and learn how to harness it to power simple devices. Get ready for an exciting journey into the world of solar power!

Materials Needed:

- Solar panel or solar cell (can be purchased online or at a science store)
- Small DC motor
- LED light
- Wires with alligator clips
- Multimeter (optional for advanced measurements)
- Sunlight or a bright lamp
- Cardboard or wooden base
- Hot glue gun or adhesive tape
- Safety goggles (optional but recommended)

Experiment Steps:

Step 1: Set Up Your Workspace

Place your cardboard or wooden base on a flat surface. Make sure you have all your materials organized and ready to use. Wear safety goggles if handling tools like hot glue guns.

Step 2: Connect the Solar Panel to the DC Motor

Take your solar panel or solar cell and identify the positive (+) and negative (-) terminals. Use the wires with alligator clips to connect the solar panel to the DC motor. Clip one wire to the positive terminal of the solar panel and the other wire to the positive terminal of the DC motor. Repeat the process for the negative terminals.

Step 3: Test the Solar Power

Position your solar panel so that it receives direct sunlight, or use a bright lamp as a substitute. Watch as the sunlight hits the solar panel and activates the DC motor. The motor begins spinning, showcasing the conversion of solar energy into mechanical energy.

Step 4: Add an LED Light

Now, let's add another component to our solar-powered system. Connect an LED light to the DC motor using the wires with alligator clips. Clip one wire to the LED light's positive terminal and the other to the negative terminal. Position the LED light so that it is facing you.

Step 5: Observe the Light

Once again, expose the solar panel to sunlight or bright light. As the solar panel generates electricity from the light, the DC motor will spin and power the LED light. Observe how the LED light turns on, demonstrating how solar energy is converted into electrical energy to illuminate a light bulb.

Step 6: Measure Power Output (Optional)

Those interested in more advanced measurements can use a multimeter to measure the voltage and current produced by the solar panel. Connect the multimeter to the terminals of the solar panel and observe the readings as sunlight hits the panel. This will give you a better understanding of solar energy's power output.

Step 7: Experiment with Angles and Light Intensity

Try tilting the solar panel at different angles to see how it affects the power output. You can also vary the distance between the light source and the solar panel to observe how light intensity impacts energy generation. Experimenting with these variables will help you learn more about optimizing solar energy capture.

You've completed an exciting experiment exploring solar energy and its conversion into electricity. Reflect on what you've learned about harnessing the sun's power and how solar energy is a clean and sustainable power source for various applications. Keep exploring and experimenting with renewable energy to unlock more mysteries of science!

Experiment 2: Wind Energy

Wind energy is a renewable and clean source of power that comes from the movement of air. In this experiment, we will explore how wind energy works and learn how to harness it to generate electricity. Get ready for an exciting journey into the world of wind power!

Materials Needed:

- Pinwheel or small wind turbine kit (can be purchased online or at a science store)
- DC motor or small generator
- LED light or small bulb
- Wires with alligator clips
- Fan or hairdryer (to simulate wind)
- Multimeter (optional for advanced measurements)

- Cardboard or wooden base

- Hot glue gun or adhesive tape

- Safety goggles (optional but recommended)

Experiment Steps:

Step 1: Set Up Your Workspace

Place your cardboard or wooden base on a flat surface. Ensure you have all your materials organized and ready to use. Remember to wear safety goggles for protection using tools like hot glue guns.

Step 2: Assemble the Wind Turbine

If you're using a pinwheel or wind turbine kit, carefully follow the instructions to assemble it. Attach the blades securely to the turbine's hub, ensuring they are evenly spaced and aligned for balanced rotation. Make sure the turbine can spin freely without any obstruction.

Step 3: Connect the Wind Turbine to the Generator

Attach the DC motor or small generator to the base using hot glue or adhesive tape. Connect one end of the wires with alligator clips to the generator terminals. Clip the other end of the wires to the

LED light or small bulb, ensuring you match the positive and negative terminals correctly.

Step 4: Test the Wind Turbine

Position the wind turbine before a fan or use a hairdryer set to the lowest setting to simulate wind. Direct the airflow towards the turbine's blades and observe as they spin. As the blades rotate, the generator will produce electricity, lighting up the LED or small bulb, indicating successful energy generation.

Step 5: Measure Power Output (Optional)

Those interested in more advanced measurements can use a multimeter to measure the generator's voltage and current. Connect the multimeter to the generator's terminals and observe the readings as the blades spin. This will give you a better understanding of wind energy's power output.

Step 6: Experiment with Wind Speed

Adjust the speed of the fan or hairdryer to see how it affects the rotation of the turbine blades and the power output. Note how stronger winds produce more electricity, demonstrating the relationship between wind speed and energy generation.

Step 7: Explore Blade Design

Experiment with different blade designs for your wind turbine. Use cardboard or plastic to create blades of varying lengths, shapes, and angles. Observe how each blade design impacts the turbine's performance and energy generation. Discuss with your young scientists which blade design is most efficient and why.

Step 8: Discuss Applications of Wind Energy

Take some time to discuss the various applications of wind energy in the real world with your young scientists. Discuss wind farms, where multiple wind turbines are connected to generate electricity on a larger scale. Also, discuss how wind energy contributes to sustainable and environmentally friendly power generation.

Now that you've made these discoveries, take some time to reflect on what you've learned about harnessing the power of the wind and how wind energy is a clean and renewable energy source. Keep exploring and experimenting with renewable energy to unlock more mysteries of energy!

Chapter Six: Sports and Science

Have you ever marveled at the fluidity of Olympic swimmers as they slice through the water like sleek dolphins? Or have you wondered about the precise movements that go into a golfer's perfect swing, sending the ball soaring across lush green fairways? And let's not forget the awe-inspiring feats of track and field athletes, whose speed and strength seem almost superhuman as they break records and push boundaries.

This chapter will peek behind the scenes and reveal the hard science that makes these marvelous sports moments so interesting. We will peel back the puzzles of hydrodynamics, discovering how water resistance affects swimmers' performance and understanding the streamlined techniques they utilize to secure a competitive edge. You will learn the physics of the golf swing, from the club's angle of impact to the body's rotation, which is responsible for the perfect swing that results in a hole-in-one.

But that's not all! Furthermore, we will have a short sprint into the world of track and field, discussing the biomechanics of running, jumping, and throwing. Every move is a fabulous amalgamation of science and athleticism, from the electrifying power of sprinters' muscles to the precision of a high jumper's takeoff.

Lace up your running shoes, put on your swimming cap, and let's learn about the science behind sports' magic!

Story 1: The Science Behind the Perfect Swing

When people think of baseball's great past, few names come to mind as much as Babe Ruth's. Born George Herman Ruth Jr. on February 6, 1895, in Baltimore, Maryland, Babe Ruth became a baseball player and a living hero. He changed the game and people's views on it forever.

Young George Herman, or "Babe" as he would be known, grew up in a working-class neighborhood where the echoes of baseball games resonated through the streets. It was here, amidst the sound of cracking bats and cheering crowds, that Babe's love affair with baseball began.

As a child, Babe Ruth showed a natural talent for the game. He could hit a ball farther and harder than anyone his age, and his pitching arm seemed blessed with otherworldly accuracy. It wasn't long before local coaches and scouts noticed the young prodigy's skills.

At the early age of 19, Babe Ruth was signed by the Boston Red Sox, marking the beginning of a remarkable career that would span over two decades and redefine the game of baseball.

Babe Ruth was a fantastic baseball player because he didn't just hit the ball with strength; he used science to make his swings even better! Imagine swinging a bat like Babe Ruth did. When he turned, he used his whole body to generate power. He knew he could hit the ball hard if he twisted his hips and swung the bat fast.

First, let's talk about momentum and torque. These are big words, but they're all about how things move. When Babe Ruth swung his bat, he didn't just use his arms. He used his whole body!

Imagine you're on a swing at the playground. When you push the swing hard, it goes higher and faster, right? That's because you gave it a lot of energy, just like Babe Ruth did when he swung his baseball bat. This energy that makes things move faster and stronger is called momentum.

Now, let's talk about torque. Have you ever tried opening a jar of pickles? Sometimes, it's hard to turn the lid because it's tight. You use torque when you use your strength to twist the lid and open the jar. Torque is like the twisting force that helps you open the jar or turn a doorknob.

When Babe Ruth swung his bat, he didn't just use his arms. He used his whole body, twisting his hips and shoulders to generate much power. This twisting motion created torque, adding even more strength to his swing. It's like tightening a rubber band before letting it go—it has a lot of force when you release it!

So, in baseball, momentum, and torque are important because they help players hit the ball harder and farther. By understanding these concepts, players like Babe Ruth were able to master the science behind hitting and become great hitters.

Next, let's talk about bat speed. Bat speed is how fast the bat moves through the air when it hits the ball. The quicker the bat moves, the more energy it transfers to the ball. Imagine swinging a bat slowly versus swinging it as fast as you can. Which one do you think will hit the ball farther? The quicker the bat moves when it hits the ball, the farther it will go! Babe Ruth practiced swinging fast to ensure he could powerfully hit the ball.

Babe Ruth also understood the importance of timing and precision. Timing is knowing when to swing the bat to hit the ball just right, and precision is hitting the ball in the sweet spot—the part of the bat that sends the ball flying! Babe Ruth practiced his timing and precision daily to ensure he could hit the ball with power and accuracy.

Now, let's discuss the shape of the bat and aerodynamics. When we discuss the shape of the bat and aerodynamics, we dive into how the bat helps players hit the ball effectively. It's not just a simple stick; it's a carefully crafted tool that can make a big difference in the game.

Let's start with the shape of the bat. Have you ever noticed that baseball bats are round and have a thicker barrel? This design isn't just for looks; it helps players make solid contact with the ball. When Babe Ruth swung his bat, he didn't just aim to hit the ball straight on. He also used a technique called backspin.

Backspin occurs when the player hits the ball, causing it to spin backward. Imagine spinning a top and watching it spin smoothly on its axis. That's similar to hitting a baseball with a backspin. This spinning motion creates lift, just like an airplane wing. The lift helps the ball stay in the air longer and travel farther, making it harder for fielders to catch. So, hitting the ball with a backspin is a crucial skill in baseball, and players like Babe Ruth mastered this technique to hit home runs.

Now, let's talk about bat weight and length. Babe Ruth wanted more than just any bat; he experimented with different weights and lengths to find the perfect balance. He discovered that a slightly heavier bat gave him more power. Imagine swinging a heavier object; it takes more force, but the impact is more substantial when you connect. However, swinging a heavy bat requires more effort and can slow down your swing speed.

On the other hand, a lighter bat is more manageable and can swing quickly. It allows for faster bat speed, which can help you hit the ball with precision and react to different pitches. However, a lighter bat may have less power behind it, so finding the right balance between control and speed is crucial.

Ultimately, Babe Ruth chose a bat that perfectly balanced power and speed. He understood how the bat's shape, weight, and length affect how he hits the ball and how far it travels. By mastering these aspects of bat design and aerodynamics, players like Babe Ruth excelled in hitting and left a lasting impact on baseball.

Now, let's put it all together. When Babe Ruth stepped up to the plate, he used his whole body to generate power. He twisted his hips and shoulders to create torque, swung the bat fast for momentum, and timed his swing just right for precision. The bat's shape and weight added spin to the ball, helping him hit it far into the outfield.

So, hitting a baseball like Babe Ruth combines science, timing, precision, and practice. It's not just about swinging hard; it's about understanding how to use your body and the bat to make the ball fly!

While Babe Ruth's physical abilities were extraordinary, his mental approach to hitting was equally impressive. He had unwavering confidence in his skills and approached every at-bat with a focused, determined mindset.

Ruth's mental toughness was evident in his ability to perform under pressure. Whether it was a crucial game-winning hit or a high-pressure situation with runners on base, Ruth remained calm and composed, relying on his years of experience and knowledge of the game to deliver when it mattered most.

However, the most critical component of Ruth's mental game was his understanding of the psychology of baseball. This was possibly the most important aspect altogether. He was well aware that baseball was a cerebral battle in addition to a physical one, and he used this understanding to his advantage all during the game. The body language of pitchers was something that Ruth would frequently observe, hoping for small indications that would reveal the pitcher's next delivery. His acute sense of observation enabled him to anticipate pitches and gain an advantage over pitchers from the other team.

Babe Ruth had an effect on baseball that went beyond his impressive records and statistics. He changed how batters played the game by introducing a scientific way of hitting that still affects players today.

Ruth's legacy isn't just the number of home runs he hit or the records he set; it's also how he changed how people hit the ball. He hit the ball with power, accuracy, and strategy in a way never seen before. He set a new bar for baseball greatness.

One of Ruth's most important achievements in the sport was a scientific explanation of how the perfect swing works. It wasn't enough for him to simply swing the bat with a lot of force; he also studied how to hit the ball and continued to improve his technique. Ruth's ability to hit the ball with excellent accuracy and power directly resulted from his ability to utilize motion, torque, and bat speed to his advantage.

He was one of the best baseball players of all time, and his records, such as the most home runs in a season and the highest career slugging percentage, stood for decades. But Ruth's impact went beyond what he did on the field. He taught generations of players to think like scientists about the game, study the details of playing, and always try to be the best.

Young baseball players still study Babe Ruth's swing to learn how it works and what they can learn from it. Coaches and teachers emphasize the importance of good technique, speed, and bat control, all of which can be traced back to how Ruth hit.

Baseball has changed thanks to better technology and training methods, but the basics of hitting that Babe Ruth learned still apply today. Understanding how to make power, control the bat, and make exact contact with the ball is as old as the game itself. It's called the "perfect swing."

As we remember Babe Ruth's story, we can see that to be successful in baseball (and life), you must be talented, work hard, and know the basics. He changed the sport in a way that will be felt for many years, pushing new players to be the best and approach the game with a scientific mind.

Story 2: Swimming With Science

Emily was absolutely captivated by the water and the sport of swimming when she was a very small child. After spending many hours frolicking in the water, she was eager to discover the techniques that would allow her to glide through the water smoothly.

Emily's parents took her to the neighborhood swimming pool on a bright and beautiful day so that she could have her first swimming lesson. A surge of pleasure and anticipation rushed through her as she put her toes into the refreshing water beneath her feet. The swimming teacher, Sarah, introduced herself, smiled, and began instructing her in the fundamentals of swimming strokes.

Emily's journey into swimming began with excitement and curiosity. Still, as she entered the water for her first swimming lesson, she quickly realized swimming was more challenging than it looked. She struggled to coordinate her movements and stay afloat, often splashing and flailing in frustration. However, Coach Sarah was there to guide her with patience and encouragement.

Coach Sarah explained to Emily that swimming is about moving through the water and understanding the science behind it. She introduced Emily to fluid dynamics, which is all about how liquids, like water, move and interact with objects in their path.

One of the first things Coach Sarah taught Emily was about water resistance. Water resistance is the force that opposes the motion of an object through water. Coach Sarah explained that when Emily moved her arms and legs in the water, she pushed against this resistance, slowing her down.

To help Emily improve her swimming, Coach Sarah taught her about streamlining. Streamlining reduces drag, or resistance, by aligning the body so water flows smoothly around it. Coach Sarah showed Emily how to keep her body straight, tuck in her chin, and extend her arms and legs to create a streamlined shape, similar to a torpedo.

As Emily practiced streamlining, she noticed she could move through the water more smoothly and swiftly. Reducing drag allowed her to glide through the water with less effort, making her strokes more efficient.

Coach Sarah also introduced Emily to the concept of hydrodynamics, the study of how water moves and the forces it exerts on objects in motion. She explained how different swimming techniques, such as the freestyle and butterfly strokes, manipulate water flow to propel the swimmer forward.

For example, Coach Sarah showed Emily how the freestyle stroke involves reaching forward with one arm while pulling the other back through the water. This motion creates a powerful thrust that propels the swimmer forward. Similarly, the butterfly stroke uses a dolphin-like motion to efficiently generate thrust and move through the water.

Emily was fascinated by how slight adjustments in her arm and leg movements could significantly improve her speed and agility in the water. She practiced different swimming techniques and experimented with her strokes to see how they affected her movement.

With this new information, Emily practiced diligently every day to improve. She worked on improving her swimming skills by trying different breathing methods and changing how her body moves to reduce resistance. Emily was driven and strong, even though there were problems and setbacks. She knew practice and persistence were the keys to improving as a swimmer.

Emily worked hard for weeks and months, and it paid off. She felt better about herself and improved her swimming. Soon, she could glide through the pool with ease and speed. She stood out from her peers because she worked hard to learn and use fluid dynamics in her swimming.

One sunny afternoon, Emily participated in her first swimming competition. The pool echoed with cheers and applause as she dived into the water, showcasing her improved strokes and techniques. With each lap, Emily felt the thrill of the water rushing past her, propelling her forward with each powerful stroke.

As Emily reached the finish line, she looked up at the scoreboard in amazement. She had finished the race and set a new personal best time! Coach Sarah beamed with pride as she congratulated Emily on her achievement. "You did it, Emily!" she exclaimed. "Your dedication, practice, and understanding of fluid dynamics have made you a better swimmer."

From that day on, Emily continued to pursue her passion for swimming with renewed vigor and enthusiasm. She understood that swimming was about moving through the water and mastering the science behind it. With each stroke, Emily embraced the joy of swimming and the power of practice and perseverance, inspiring others to dive into the world of swimming with confidence and curiosity.

The science behind Emily's improved swimming skills lies in fluid dynamics, the study of how liquids and gases move and interact with objects in their path. Understanding fluid dynamics helps swimmers minimize resistance and maximize propulsion, allowing them to move more efficiently through the water.

One of the critical concepts of fluid dynamics in swimming is hydrodynamics, which focuses on the forces and pressures water exerts on a moving object. When swimmers move through the water, they encounter resistance, which slows them down. By minimizing resistance through proper body positioning and technique, swimmers can move faster with less effort.

Streamlining is another crucial aspect of fluid dynamics in swimming. It reduces drag by aligning the body so water flows smoothly around it. Swimmers often tuck in their chin, keep their bodies straight, and extend their arms and legs to create a streamlined shape, similar to a torpedo. This reduces the resistance encountered and helps swimmers move faster through the water.

The shape and design of swimming strokes also affect fluid dynamics. Different strokes, such as freestyle, backstroke, breaststroke, and butterfly, utilize varying techniques to maximize propulsion and minimize resistance. For example, the butterfly stroke involves a dolphin-like motion that generates powerful thrust, while the breaststroke emphasizes a frog-like kick to move through the water efficiently.

Breathing techniques are another aspect of fluid dynamics that swimmers must master. Proper breathing provides oxygen to the muscles and helps swimmers maintain their body position and streamline. Swimmers often coordinate their breathing with their strokes, exhaling underwater and inhaling quickly when their head is above water.

As Emily learned and applied these fluid dynamics principles to her swimming, she noticed significant improvements in her speed, endurance, and overall performance. She realized she could become a more efficient and skilled swimmer by understanding the science behind swimming.

Emily's journey also taught her valuable lessons about practice and perseverance. She learned that progress takes time and effort and that setbacks are opportunities to learn and grow. Through dedication and determination, Emily transformed from a novice swimmer to a confident athlete, inspiring others with her passion for swimming and understanding of its science.

Story 3: The Race Against Time

In the heart of a bustling city, a young athlete named Alex dreamed of becoming the fastest runner in the world. Excitement, challenges, and a deep dive into the fascinating world of sports science filled Alex's journey.

Coach Maya's sports science knowledge helped Alex a lot on his way to becoming a world-class runner. Biomechanics is one of the most essential parts of sports science, and it has helped us learn and improve Alex's running technique.

Biomechanics is like a magic wand that helps scientists understand how the body moves while doing different things, like running. They look like they have a particular pair of glasses that let them see how things move. Using high-tech cameras and sensors, Coach Maya used this tool to keep track of Alex's running moves.

During these biomechanical studies, Coach Maya and Alex examined a few essential parts of Alex's running form. One of the first things they checked was stride length, or how far Alex's legs spread with each step. Coach Maya saw that Alex's stride length was sometimes wrong, too short or too long. She worked with Alex to help him find the best stride length for speed and economy.

Another important factor was the placement of the feet. Coach Maya saw Alex's feet falling too far apart, making them move sideways and slow down. Coach Maya taught Alex to land with their feet closer together by looking at their biomechanics. This made their push-off stronger and more efficient with every step.

Coach Maya saw Alex's arms swinging too far apart, making the air fight him too much. This was making Alex move more slowly and waste energy. Coach Maya told Alex to keep their arms closer to their bodies while they ran to fix the problem. This change improved the airflow, enabling Alex to move faster with less effort.

Coach Maya helped Alex reach their full running potential by making these small but essential changes based on physical knowledge. Getting Alex to run with the proper stride length, foot placement, and arm swings changed how they ran, making them faster, better, and more efficient on the track. The fact that this change happened shows how powerful sports science is and how it can improve athletic ability.

But running isn't just about moving your legs and arms—it's also about breathing and staying relaxed. Coach Maya introduced Alex to the science of sports psychology, which focuses on the mental aspect of sports. They practiced visualization techniques, where Alex would close their eyes and imagine themselves running smoothly and effortlessly. This helped Alex stay calm and focused during races, even during tough competition.

Nutrition played a crucial role in Alex's training regimen, ensuring they had the energy and nutrients needed to perform at their best. Coach Maya collaborated with a sports nutritionist to design a personalized meal plan tailored to Alex's needs and goals.

The meal plan focused on providing Alex with a well-balanced diet with the right macronutrients: proteins, carbohydrates, and fats. Lean proteins, such as chicken and fish, were included to support muscle repair and growth, which is essential for recovering from intense workouts and building strength.

Complex carbohydrates were another essential component of Alex's diet. Whole grains and fruits provided a steady energy source, crucial for fueling long training sessions and maintaining endurance during races.

Additionally, healthy fats played a vital role in Alex's nutrition plan. Foods like avocados and nuts provide essential fatty acids supporting overall health, including heart and brain function.

By following this nutrition plan, Alex ensured they were getting the proper nutrients in the right proportions to optimize performance, aid recovery, and maintain overall well-being throughout their training and competitions.

As Alex's training progressed, Coach Maya introduced them to the concept of interval training. This involved alternating between periods of high-intensity running and rest. Interval training helped Alex build endurance and speed, making them a more substantial and faster runner overall.

On race day, Alex was physically and mentally prepared. They used visualization techniques to stay focused and confident. As they crossed the finish line, breaking the world record, Alex knew that their journey through sports science had played a crucial role in achieving their dream.

Through Alex's story, kids can learn that sports isn't just about natural talent—it's also about understanding how the body works, staying mentally strong, and fueling it with the proper nutrition. It shows that with dedication, hard work, and the help of science, anyone can achieve their goals, whether it's in sports or any other aspect of life.

Experiment 1:

This experiment aims to learn about the dynamics of hitting a bat and how different factors affect the bat's motion and speed.

Materials Needed:

- A baseball bat
- Baseball or softball
- Stopwatch or timer
- Tape measure or marked distance
- Open outdoor space or a large room with a high ceiling

Instructions:

Step 1: Set it Up

Set up the experiment area in an open outdoor space or a large room with a high ceiling where it's safe to swing a bat without obstructions.

Step 2: Mark Your Start Point

Mark a starting point on the ground or floor using a tape measure or marked distance. This will be the spot from where you'll swing the bat.

Step 3: Grip the Bat

Hold the baseball bat correctly, with both hands gripping the handle and the barrel facing away from you.

Step 4: Prepare and Practice

Stand at the starting point and swing the bat like you're hitting a baseball. Try to swing with the same force and speed each time.

Step 5: Time Yourself

Have a partner or parent tell you how long it takes for the bat to complete the swing, starting when you initiate it and ending when the bat stops moving.

Step 6: Repeat

Repeat the swinging motion multiple times to keep the force and speed consistent.

Step 7: Measure

Measure the distance covered by the bat during each swing. You can use a tape measure or simply mark the bat's landing spot and measure the distance afterward.

Record your results, including the time taken for each swing and the distance the bat covers.

Now, change one variable at a time and observe how it affects the bat's motion:

a. Change the grip on the bat (e.g., hold it tighter or looser) and see if it affects the swing speed.

b. Change the bat's weight by adding or removing weight (e.g., by tapping on coins or removing some of the bat's weight) and observe the difference in swing speed and distance covered.

c. Experiment with swinging the bat at different angles (e.g., level swing, upward swing, downward swing) and observe how the trajectory and distance change.

d. Try swinging the bat with different amounts of force and observe how it affects the speed and the distance the bat covers.

After completing the experiment and recording your observations, analyze the results to see how different factors influenced the dynamics of hitting the bat. Discuss with your partner or parent what you learned about bat dynamics, including how grip, weight, angle of swing, and force affect the bat's motion and speed.

This experiment helps you understand the dynamics of hitting a bat and how various factors influence the bat's motion and speed. By exploring different variables, you can gain insights into the physics principles of hitting a bat and apply this knowledge to improve your batting skills in baseball or softball.

Conclusion

Throughout this book, we've embarked on a thrilling journey through the wonders of science, exploring the vast realms of space and the mysteries of our planet, delving into the fascinating world of living things, uncovering the ingenious inventions and the brilliant minds behind them, harnessing the incredible power of energy, and diving deep into the captivating realm of sports science. As we conclude our journey, let's reflect on what we've learned and our incredible discoveries.

We've marveled at its beauty and vastness in exploring space and the universe. We've also learned about comets, Mars explorations, and the extent of our solar system!

Our journey also took us to the wonders of our planet, Earth. We've learned about the diverse ecosystems, the intricate balance of nature, and the importance of preserving our environment. From the depths of the oceans to the heights of mountains, we've discovered the incredible diversity of life on Earth and the delicate harmony that sustains it.

Through our exploration of living things, we've delved into the fascinating world of biology. We've learned about the different species of plants and animals, the ecosystems they inhabit, and the unique adaptations that allow them to thrive in their environments. From the tiniest microorganisms to the majestic creatures of the animal kingdom, we've marveled at the complexity and beauty of life.

Our journey would only be complete with celebrating the incredible inventions and the ingenious inventors who have shaped our world. We've learned about the transformative power of human creativity and innovation from the wheel to the internet. We've explored the inventions that have changed how we live, work, and communicate, and the visionaries who dared to dream big and make their ideas a reality all inspire us.

Our energy exploration has taken us on a quest to understand the different forms of energy, from solar to wind power and nuclear. We've learned about renewable energy sources and explored the importance of energy conservation and sustainability. We've discovered how energy powers our world and fuels our daily lives and gained a deeper appreciation for the need to use energy wisely and responsibly.

Finally, our journey into sports science has opened our eyes to the fascinating intersection of science and athletics. We've learned about sports physics, biomechanics of movement, and the role of nutrition and psychology in athletic performance. We've discovered how science can help athletes push the boundaries of human potential and achieve extraordinary feats.

As we conclude our journey through science, let's remember that curiosity and exploration are the keys to unlocking the secrets of the universe and the wonders of our world. Whether we're gazing at the stars, studying the intricacies of life, marveling at human ingenuity, harnessing the power of energy, or pushing our physical limits through sport, science invites us to ask questions, seek answers, and embark on endless adventures of discovery. So, let's continue to explore, learn, and be inspired by the incredible world of science!

Bonus Experiments

Bonus Experiment 1: Balloon Rocket Science

Have you ever wondered how rockets launch into space? Rockets use powerful forces to push themselves off the ground and into the sky. In this experiment, we will create our own mini-rocket using a balloon and explore how air can be used to propel objects forward. Get ready to blast off and learn about the science behind rockets!

Be sure to ask a parent or guardian to join you and help you with this experiment. Safety first!

Materials Needed:

- Balloon
- String
- Drinking straw
- Tape
- Scissors

Experiment Steps:

Step 1: Set Up the Rocket Path

Start by threading the string through the straw. This straw will act as the guide for your balloon rocket. Next, tape one end of the string to a sturdy surface, like a chair or door handle, and stretch the string tightly across the room. Tape the other end to another object, keeping it high enough to create a straight path for the balloon.

Step 2: Prepare the Rocket

Blow up a balloon but don't tie it. Hold the open end of the balloon while taping it to the straw. Make sure the balloon's open end is facing backward, so the air can escape.

Step 3: Launch the Rocket

Let go of the balloon and watch it shoot along the string as air escapes! Notice how the balloon moves forward as the air pushes out of the opening.

Step 4: Experiment with Different Designs

Try changing the size or shape of the balloon. Does a larger balloon travel farther? What happens if you launch two balloons at once? Test different ideas to see how they affect your rocket's performance.

Step 5: Try Different String Lengths

Use a shorter or longer string and see how that changes the speed of the balloon rocket. Does a longer string slow it down?

Step 6: Test Air Pressure

Experiment with how much air you put into the balloon. How does the amount of air affect how far and how fast the balloon goes?

Step 7: Discuss and Reflect

Talk about what you observed during the experiment. What made the balloon rocket move? How does the air inside the balloon help push it forward? This simple experiment is a demonstration of Newton's Third Law of Motion: For every action, there is an equal and opposite reaction. In the case of the balloon, the action is the air pushing out, and the reaction is the balloon moving forward.

You've now learned the basics of how rockets launch! Keep experimenting with different variables and see how they affect your balloon's speed and distance. The sky's the limit!

Bonus Experiment 2: Homemade Lava Lamp

Lava lamps are mesmerizing because they create moving blobs of color that seem to float and dance. But how do they work? In this experiment, you'll create your own lava lamp and discover how oil and water interact, along with the exciting effect of adding Alka-Seltzer. Prepare to be amazed by the bubbling magic!

Materials Needed:

- Clear bottle or jar
- Water
- Vegetable oil or baby oil
- Food coloring
- Alka-Seltzer tablet

Experiment Steps:

Step 1: Prepare Your Bottle

Fill your clear bottle or jar about halfway with water. This will form the base of your homemade lava lamp.

Step 2: Add Oil

Carefully pour vegetable or baby oil into the bottle until it's almost full. You'll notice the oil floats on top of the water instead of mixing with it.

Step 3: Add Color

Drop 5-10 drops of food coloring into the bottle. The food coloring will sink through the oil and mix with the water, creating a colorful effect.

Step 4: Create the Lava Effect

Break an Alka-Seltzer tablet into smaller pieces. Drop one piece into the bottle and watch as it starts to bubble, pushing colorful blobs through the oil.

Step 5: Continue the Fun

Once the bubbling stops, you can add more Alka-Seltzer pieces to keep your lava lamp active. Each time, new bubbles will rise and fall through the oil and water.

Step 6: Experiment with Different Colors

Try using different colors of food coloring. You can mix them to create new colors or stick with a single color for a more uniform look. What happens if you add two Alka-Seltzer tablets at once?

Step 7: Observe and Discuss

Talk about why the oil and water don't mix. Oil is less dense than water, so it floats on top. The Alka-Seltzer reacts with the water to create carbon dioxide bubbles, which rise through the oil, taking colorful water with them. As the bubbles pop, the water sinks back down.

Discuss and Reflect:

What did you notice about the movement of the colored water in the oil? Why do the bubbles rise and fall? By making this lava lamp, you've explored how liquids of different densities behave and how chemical reactions can create movement. Keep experimenting by trying different oils, adding more tablets, or changing the amounts of water and oil.

Enjoy your colorful creation!

Bonus Experiment 3: Static Electricity Butterfly

Static electricity can be used to make objects move without touching them! In this experiment, you'll make a paper butterfly and use static electricity to make its wings move, simulating how static electricity can exert a force from a distance. Let's see how electricity and air can make the wings come alive!

Materials Needed:

- Tissue paper
- Balloon
- Tape
- Scissors

Experiment Steps:

Step 1: Cut Out a Butterfly

Use scissors to cut a butterfly shape out of tissue paper. You can make it as big or small as you like, but remember, lighter wings will move more easily.

Step 2: Tape the Butterfly Down

Tape the center of the butterfly to a smooth surface, like a table or a piece of cardboard. Leave the wings free to move.

Step 3: Create Static Electricity

Blow up a balloon and rub it on your hair or a wool sweater to create static electricity. Keep rubbing the balloon for 10–15 seconds.

Step 4: Bring the Balloon Close

Hold the balloon near the wings of the butterfly without touching them. Watch the wings react to the static charge!

Step 5: Move the Balloon

Slowly move the balloon closer and farther away from the butterfly's wings and see how it affects the movement. Can you make the wings flutter without touching them?

Step 6: Experiment with Distance

Try holding the balloon at different distances from the butterfly. How close does the balloon need to be for the wings to move? What happens when you move the balloon too far away?

Step 7: Discuss and Reflect

Why do the wings move when the balloon gets close? When you rub the balloon on your hair, it gains an electric charge. This charge attracts the tissue paper, making the wings move. This is a fun way to explore static electricity and the forces it creates!

Enjoy experimenting with the power of static electricity to make your butterfly wings flutter!

Bonus Experiment 4: Invisible Ink

In this experiment, you'll learn how to write secret messages using invisible ink! With just a few simple ingredients, you'll create a message that's completely invisible until revealed with heat. This is a fun way to explore the science of chemical reactions and how substances change with temperature.

Materials Needed:

- Lemon juice
- Q-tip or paintbrush
- White paper
- Lamp or light bulb

Experiment Steps:

Step 1: Create the Ink

Squeeze a lemon into a small bowl to collect the juice. You can add a little water if needed to thin the juice.

Step 2: Write Your Message

Dip the Q-tip or paintbrush into the lemon juice and write a secret message on the white paper. Let the paper dry completely so the message becomes invisible.

Step 3: Prepare the Heat Source

Turn on a lamp with a regular light bulb. Make sure you have a safe area to heat the paper.

Step 4: Reveal the Message

Hold the paper close to the light bulb but not too close to avoid burning. As the paper heats up, the message will begin to appear!

Step 5: Experiment with Other Liquids

Try using other liquids like milk or vinegar to see if they work as invisible ink. Do different liquids reveal better or faster?

Step 6: Try Different Heat Sources

Instead of a lamp, you can try using a candle or other heat source to reveal your message. Just make sure to keep a safe distance from open flames.

Step 7: Discuss and Reflect

What makes the invisible ink appear? The heat causes the lemon juice to oxidize and turn brown, revealing the message. This chemical reaction is an exciting way to learn about the effects of heat on substances!

Have fun sharing your secret messages with friends and family!

Bonus Experiment 5: Build a Simple Compass

In this experiment, you will create a simple compass using a few household items. This compass will help you locate magnetic north, just like a real one! This is a fun and easy way to learn about magnetism and how the Earth's magnetic field works.

Materials Needed:
- Sewing needle
- Magnet
- Bowl of water
- Cork or piece of Styrofoam

Experiment Steps:

Step 1: Magnetize the Needle

Take the magnet and rub it along the length of the needle in one direction about 30 times. This process magnetizes the needle, allowing it to interact with Earth's magnetic field.

Step 2: Prepare the Floating Device

Cut a small piece of cork or Styrofoam to float the needle. Carefully push the needle through the center of the cork so that it stays straight.

Step 3: Place the Compass in Water

Fill a bowl with water and gently place the cork with the needle on the water's surface. The needle will align itself with Earth's magnetic field and point toward magnetic north.

Step 4: Test the Compass

Turn the bowl slowly and watch as the needle moves to realign itself with magnetic north.

Step 5: Experiment with Different Sizes

Try using different sizes of needles or other metal objects. Do they work as well as the needle?

Step 6: Try Other Magnetic Materials

Instead of a magnet, experiment with items that might have a magnetic field (e.g., refrigerator magnets). Do these work to magnetize the needle?

Step 7: Discuss and Reflect

How did your homemade compass work? By magnetizing the needle, you created a simple compass that reacts to Earth's magnetic field. This is how real compasses help us navigate by pointing north!

Now you have your own tool for exploration—happy navigating!

Bonus Experiment 6: Rainbow in a Glass

Rainbows are beautiful natural phenomena caused by the refraction of light through water droplets. In this experiment, you'll create your own "rainbow" in a glass using different sugar solutions and food coloring. It's a colorful way to learn about density and how liquids with different densities behave!

Materials Needed:

- Sugar
- Water
- Food coloring (several colors)
- Spoon
- Clear glass

Experiment Steps:

Step 1: Prepare the Sugar Solutions

In four different cups, mix water with varying amounts of sugar (e.g., 1 tbsp, 2 tbsp, 3 tbsp, 4 tbsp). Add a different color of food coloring to each cup.

Step 2: Layer the Solutions

Using a spoon, carefully layer the colored sugar water in the glass, starting with the densest solution (most sugar) at the bottom and working your way to the least dense (least sugar) at the top. Pour slowly to keep the layers from mixing.

Step 3: Observe the Rainbow

Once all layers are poured, look at the beautiful rainbow you've created in the glass! The different densities keep the layers from mixing right away.

Step 4: Experiment with Layering

Try using different amounts of sugar or different colors of food coloring. Can you make the layers more distinct? What happens if you pour faster or slower?

Step 5: Try Hot and Cold Water

See if temperature affects the layering by using warm water for some layers and cold water for others.

Step 6: Mix the Rainbow

After observing your layered rainbow, gently stir the glass. What happens to the colors when the layers mix? Why do they blend together?

Step 7: Discuss and Reflect

What did you learn about density? The sugar water solutions have different densities based on how much sugar they contain, which is why they create separate layers. Density plays a key role in many natural phenomena, including how rainbows form in the sky!

Enjoy experimenting with your own rainbow in a glass!

Bonus Experiment 7: Salt Crystal Garden

Crystals are beautiful and fascinating natural structures. In this experiment, you will grow your own crystals using salt and observe how they form over time. This is a great way to learn about evaporation and how minerals form crystals in nature.

Materials Needed:

- Charcoal briquettes or porous rocks
- Table salt
- Water
- Food coloring
- A shallow dish or plate

Experiment Steps:

Step 1: Prepare the Base

Place the charcoal briquettes or porous rocks in the shallow dish. These will serve as the base on which your crystals will grow.

Step 2: Mix the Solution

In a separate bowl, mix equal parts salt and water to create a saltwater solution. Stir until as much salt as possible has dissolved.

Step 3: Add Color (Optional)

If you want colorful crystals, add a few drops of food coloring to the saltwater solution and stir.

Step 4: Pour the Solution

Slowly pour the saltwater solution over the charcoal or rocks, making sure to cover them fully. Place the dish in a sunny spot or a warm, dry area.

Step 5: Observe the Crystal Formation

Over the next few days, observe how the water evaporates and leaves behind salt crystals. You'll see tiny crystals form on the surface of the rocks or charcoal.

Step 6: Experiment with Other Solutions

Try using different types of salt (e.g., Epsom salt or sea salt) and see how the crystals form differently. Does the size or shape of the crystals change?

Step 7: Discuss and Reflect

What did you notice about the growth of the crystals? This experiment mimics how crystals form in nature through the process of evaporation. As the water evaporates, the salt molecules come together and form solid crystals!

Enjoy watching your very own salt crystal garden grow!

Bonus Experiment 8: Soap-Powered Boat

In this experiment, you'll make a simple boat that moves using soap! By exploring surface tension, you'll learn how soap breaks the water's surface tension and propels the boat forward. Get ready to set sail with the power of science!

Materials Needed:

- Small piece of cardboard or paper
- Dish soap
- Bowl of water
- Scissors

Experiment Steps:

Step 1: Cut Out a Boat Shape

Cut a small boat shape out of the cardboard or paper. It can be any shape you like, as long as it's flat and lightweight.

Step 2: Prepare the Water

Fill a bowl with water and place the boat on the surface. Make sure it floats freely.

Step 3: Apply the Soap

Dip a finger into the dish soap and touch the back of the boat lightly. As soon as the soap touches the water, watch what happens to the boat!

Step 4: Observe the Movement

The boat will quickly move forward as the soap breaks the surface tension of the water. This sudden movement is a fun way to see how surface tension works.

Step 5: Experiment with Different Shapes

Cut out boats in different shapes and sizes. Do certain shapes move faster or farther than others?

Step 6: Test with Other Liquids

Try using other liquids (e.g., cooking oil, shampoo) to see if they also break the surface tension and move the boat. Which liquids work the best?

Step 7: Discuss and Reflect

What caused the boat to move? Surface tension is a force that acts on the surface of liquids. The soap breaks this tension, allowing the boat to move. This is the same principle that helps some insects walk on water!

Enjoy experimenting with your soap-powered boat!

Bonus Experiment 9: Bouncy Egg Experiment

In this experiment, you'll transform a regular egg into a bouncy ball using vinegar! The acid in the vinegar will dissolve the eggshell, leaving a soft, rubbery membrane that can bounce. It's a great way to learn about chemical reactions and how acids work.

Materials Needed:

- Egg
- Vinegar
- Bowl

Experiment Steps:

Step 1: Prepare the Egg

Place an egg in a bowl. Make sure the egg is fully intact, with no cracks.

Step 2: Add Vinegar

Pour enough vinegar into the bowl to completely cover the egg. You'll notice bubbles forming on the surface of the eggshell right away.

Step 3: Let the Egg Soak

Leave the egg in the vinegar for at least 24 hours. During this time, the vinegar will dissolve the calcium carbonate in the eggshell.

Step 4: Check the Egg

After 24 hours, carefully remove the egg from the vinegar and rinse it under water. You'll see that the hard eggshell is gone, and all that's left is a rubbery membrane.

Step 5: Bounce the Egg

Gently bounce the egg on a soft surface, like a table covered with a towel. The egg will be bouncy, but be careful not to drop it too hard, or it might break!

Step 6: Experiment with Other Liquids

Try soaking an egg in other acidic liquids, like lemon juice or soda, and see if they produce the same effect. Which liquid works best?

Step 7: Discuss and Reflect

What caused the eggshell to dissolve? The acid in the vinegar reacted with the calcium carbonate in the shell, breaking it down and leaving the membrane intact. This is a fun way to explore chemical reactions!

Enjoy playing with your bouncy egg, but handle it with care!

Bonus Experiment 10: Oobleck (Non-Newtonian Fluid)

In this experiment, you'll create a strange substance called oobleck, which behaves like both a solid and a liquid! This is a fun way to explore non-Newtonian fluids, which change their state based on the pressure applied to them.

Materials Needed:

- Cornstarch
- Water
- Food coloring (optional)

Experiment Steps:

Step 1: Mix the Ingredients

In a bowl, combine 1 part water with 2 parts cornstarch. Stir the mixture until it reaches a thick, gooey consistency.

Step 2: Test the Texture

Try pressing your hand into the oobleck slowly. It will feel like a liquid. Now try slapping it quickly—what happens? You'll notice that it behaves more like a solid!

Step 3: Add Color

For extra fun, add a few drops of food coloring to your oobleck. Mix it in to create a colorful, gooey substance.

Step 4: Experiment with Pressure

Try applying different amounts of pressure to the oobleck. Press it gently, then quickly squeeze it. How does the texture change?

Step 5: Test Different Ratios

Experiment with different amounts of water and cornstarch. How does changing the ratio affect the consistency of the oobleck?

Step 6: Try Different Containers

Pour the oobleck into containers of different shapes and sizes. Does it behave differently in a wide bowl compared to a narrow cup?

Step 7: Discuss and Reflect

What makes oobleck so unusual? This non-Newtonian fluid changes its state depending on how much pressure is applied. It behaves like a solid when you apply force but flows like a liquid when left alone!

Enjoy experimenting with your amazing oobleck!

Bonus Experiment 11: Tornado in a Bottle

Tornadoes are powerful and destructive forces of nature. In this experiment, you'll create a tornado in a bottle using simple materials, allowing you to see how a vortex forms. Get ready to spin and learn about the science behind tornadoes!

Materials Needed:

- Two plastic bottles
- Water
- Duct tape
- Glitter (optional)

Experiment Steps:

Step 1: Fill the Bottle

Fill one of the plastic bottles about two-thirds full with water. Add a small amount of glitter if you want to make your tornado more visible.

Step 2: Attach the Bottles

Place the second empty bottle on top of the water-filled bottle, neck to neck, and tape them securely together with duct tape.

Step 3: Create the Tornado

Flip the bottles upside down so that the water-filled bottle is on top. Quickly swirl the bottles in a circular motion to create a vortex.

Step 4: Observe the Tornado

As the water spins, a tornado-like vortex will form in the middle of the bottle. Watch as the water rushes down into the lower bottle, simulating a tornado!

Step 5: Experiment with Different Speeds

Try swirling the bottles at different speeds. Does a faster or slower spin create a stronger tornado?

Step 6: Add More Objects

Drop small objects, like glitter or confetti, into the water and watch how they are caught in the vortex. How do they move in the spinning water?

Step 7: Discuss and Reflect

Why does the water form a tornado? This experiment demonstrates how spinning air forms a vortex, which is how real tornadoes form. The faster the spin, the stronger the vortex!

Enjoy watching your very own tornado in a bottle!

Bonus Experiment 12: Magnetic Slime

In this fun experiment, you'll make slime that can be controlled with a magnet! By mixing iron filings into your slime, you'll explore how magnetic fields can move objects. Get ready for a hands-on lesson in magnetism!

Materials Needed:

- Liquid starch
- Glue
- Iron filings

- Magnet

Experiment Steps:

Step 1: Make the Slime

Mix equal parts glue and liquid starch in a bowl until you have a smooth, stretchy slime. This will be the base for your magnetic slime.

Step 2: Add Iron Filings

Once the slime is made, add a small amount of iron filings and knead them into the slime. Make sure they are evenly distributed.

Step 3: Test with a Magnet

Hold a magnet close to the slime and watch as the slime is attracted to the magnet. Try moving the magnet around to see how the slime follows it.

Step 4: Shape the Slime

Shape the slime into different forms and observe how the magnet affects its movement. Can you make the slime move in a straight line or form a specific shape?

Step 5: Experiment with Other Magnets

Try using different types of magnets (e.g., stronger or weaker ones) to see how they interact with the slime. Which magnet works best?

Step 6: Try Different Ratios

Make new batches of slime with more or fewer iron filings. Does adding more filings make the slime more magnetic?

Step 7: Discuss and Reflect

What makes the slime move? The iron filings in the slime are attracted to the magnetic field of the magnet. This experiment shows how magnetic fields can exert a force on objects, even from a distance!

Enjoy experimenting with your magnetic slime!

Bonus Experiment 13: Walking Water

In this colorful experiment, you'll see how water can "walk" between cups using paper towels. This is a great way to learn about capillary action and how liquids move through porous materials like paper.

Materials Needed:

- 3 clear cups
- Water
- Food coloring
- Paper towels

Experiment Steps:

Step 1: Prepare the Water

Fill two cups with water and leave the third cup empty. Add a few drops of food coloring to the two cups of water to make the experiment more colorful.

Step 2: Arrange the Cups

Place the three cups in a row, with the empty cup in the middle.

Step 3: Fold the Paper Towels

Fold two paper towels into long strips. Place one end of each paper towel into the cups with water and the other end into the empty cup in the middle.

Step 4: Watch the Water Walk

Over time, the water will start to travel up the paper towels and "walk" into the empty cup. Observe how the water moves through the paper.

Step 5: Experiment with Different Colors

Try using different colors of food coloring in each cup. What happens when the colors mix in the empty cup?

Step 6: Test Different Lengths

Use longer or shorter paper towels and see how that affects the speed of the water movement. Does the length of the paper towel make a difference?

Step 7: Discuss and Reflect

Why does the water move through the paper towels? This experiment demonstrates capillary action, which allows liquids to move through porous materials. Capillary action is important in plants, where it helps water move from the roots to the leaves!

Enjoy watching your colorful water walk between cups!

Bonus Experiment 14: Grow Your Own Geode

Geodes are hollow rocks lined with crystals, and in this experiment, you'll grow your own crystal-covered geode using common materials. This is a fun way to explore how crystals form over time through a process called crystallization.

Materials Needed:

- Alum powder (available at craft stores)
- Hot water
- Clean eggshell
- Food coloring (optional)

Experiment Steps:

Step 1: Prepare the Eggshell

Take a clean eggshell and break it into halves. The inside of the shell will serve as the base for your geode.

Step 2: Dissolve the Alum Powder

In a bowl, mix hot water with alum powder, stirring until the powder dissolves completely. Add food coloring if you want colored crystals.

Step 3: Soak the Eggshell

Place the eggshell halves in the alum solution. Make sure they are fully submerged.

Step 4: Let the Crystals Form

Leave the eggshell in the solution for at least 24 hours. Over time, crystals will begin to form on the inside of the shell.

Step 5: Remove the Geode

After 24 hours, carefully remove the eggshell from the solution and let it dry. You'll see beautiful crystals lining the inside!

Step 6: Experiment with Different Conditions

Try growing crystals using different solutions, such as sugar water or salt water. How do the crystals differ from those grown with alum?

Step 7: Discuss and Reflect

What did you observe about the crystal growth? This experiment shows how minerals form crystals through a process of crystallization as the solution evaporates. You've created your very own geode!

Enjoy displaying your beautiful homemade geode!

Bonus Experiment 15: Egg Drop Challenge

In this classic science challenge, your goal is to design a structure that protects an egg from breaking when dropped from a height. This is a fun way to learn about impact resistance, energy absorption, and engineering principles. Get creative and see if you can keep your egg safe!

Materials Needed:

- An egg
- Household materials (e.g., cotton, paper, straws, tape)
- A safe drop zone (e.g., a balcony, staircase, or ladder)

Experiment Steps:

Step 1: Gather Materials

Collect various household materials that you think could protect the egg when it falls. These could include cotton balls, paper, cardboard, straws, or bubble wrap.

Step 2: Design the Structure

Think about how to cushion the egg. You could wrap it in soft materials, build a cage, or use straws to create a shock-absorbing structure. Use your creativity!

Step 3: Build the Egg Protector

Carefully construct your egg-protecting structure. Make sure the egg is securely placed inside and won't fall out during the drop.

Step 4: Test Your Design

Go to your safe drop zone and drop the egg in its protective structure from a height. Make sure to drop it from the same height for each test.

Step 5: Observe the Results

Did your egg survive the drop? If it cracked, think about what went wrong and how you could improve the design. If it stayed intact, great job!

Step 6: Modify and Retest

Try improving your design by adding or changing materials. How can you make the structure stronger or better at absorbing impact?

Step 7: Discuss and Reflect

Why did some designs work better than others? This challenge teaches you about impact resistance and how engineers design structures to absorb energy and protect delicate objects. Keep experimenting to build the ultimate egg protector!

Made in the USA
Monee, IL
29 December 2024